Rachel Cord

Confidential Investigations

Life's a Bitch.
So am I.

R. E. Conary

EQUAL
FOOTING
BOOKS

Everyone Deserves An Equal Footing

Second Edition

Life's a Bitch. So am I.

RACHEL CORD
**Confidential Investigations
Book One**

Copyright © 2015 R. E. Conary
Cover Photo © Keeweeboy | Dreamstime.com — used by permission

Equal Footing Books
ISBN: 978-0692407516

Previously published (2008) as
'Life's a Bitch. So am I.' Rachel Cord, P.I.

To Kristine,
For the inspiration

One

My CURSE PRECEDED ME into the squad room. I hate it. A dozen faces swiveled, work ceased, sound stopped. A dozen mouths gaped in slack-jawed awe. It's a reaction I get all the time. I hate it, but it's the albatross I bear.

Polite people say I'm buxom. My breasts are huge. I didn't ask to be built like an unmilked Guernsey. The weight and strain can leave me in tears. I keep promising myself I'll get them cut down to a modest C-cup. Or better yet, a B. That would be heaven. Meanwhile, they're a pain I live with; like when they don't get me the respect I feel I deserve.

The nameplate at the first occupied desk read "DET. JABLOWSKI." I didn't wait for the fat slob sitting there to force his eyes up to my face.

"Is Captain Rodecker in?"

The detective glanced at my uniformed escort before answering. I could feel him asking, *who's this bimbo?*

"Who wants to know?"

"I do." I handed him my card.

"Hey, Carson," he said turning to his neighbor. "Check this out. We got us a dickless dick."

Jabba the Hutt thought he was cute, but I'd heard it before. That and other tasteless comments. That's what I mean about no respect.

"Better than being a useless one."

I let him cogitate about which *one* I meant—in his case it could be either. I don't take crap from anyone, especially men.

Before the slob thought of a comeback, Carson got up, took my card, and read it as he came around the desk. It's a nice card. Crisp, white, high-quality cardstock. Black lettering. Engraved, not raised. It has my name, Rachel Cord, Confidential Investigations, an address and phone number. Very professional. Just like me despite my affliction. Oh, yes, one more thing—my agency motto: *"Life's a bitch. So am I."*

I don't claim originality for the phrase, but the motto fits my attitude. When I chose this business, the detective who taught me said I'd need an attitude to survive. Life's difficult at best, and at times it's downright nasty. When things get tough, I try to be tougher.

Carson's eyes went directly from my card to my eyes without a pause along the way. I raised him a rung on the evolutionary ladder.

"Is Captain Rodecker expecting you, Miss Cord?"

There was a hint of questioning emphasis on the *Miss*. I didn't see a wedding ring so maybe he was wondering if I were available. Not my type, but let him wonder.

"No, but I think he'll see me if he's in. We used to know each other."

"I'll check if he has time to see you."

Carson headed for a glass-walled office with its blinds closed. Jabba gave a last glare before pecking at his computer keyboard. Everyone else went back to doing whatever it was they were doing before I walked in. Two *ladies* handcuffed to a bench seemed to be comparing my attributes to theirs and probably discussing the business pluses of getting implants. I wanted to tell them it wasn't worth it, but, hey, who was I to judge.

Captain of Detectives Rodney Roderick "Hot Rod" Rodecker III came out of the office with a big grin on his face. He hadn't changed a whole lot since our Army days during Desert Storm: hair thinning, maturer maybe, but all in all the same rock-hard force of nature I remembered.

"Rachel Cord, it's great to see you. Come on in."

I noticed several interested stares as we went into an office half the size it needed to be and overflowing with paperwork. He closed the door and offered me coffee, then sat behind his desk as I took one of the chairs facing it.

"God, you bring back memories. Your card says you're just across the river. What took you so long to look me up?"

"Serendipity. I didn't know where you were until I read about your recent promotion. How many Rodney R. Rodeckers can there be?" Besides your father and grandfather, that is. "I don't usually work outside the city, but I needed to come over here. It seemed pleasantly fated you were here too."

"What, you don't think we're a city? We're thirty thousand strong and shrinking. " Rod flashed his grin again. "Anyway, how long's it been?"

"Twelve years. Not since you shipped out for OCS."

"Right. I remember hoping you were my going away gift."

"It wasn't in the cards, 'Hot Rod'."

He blushed and raised his hands. "Please, easy with the 'Hot Rod' stuff. I hope I've left that reputation behind. But I may have trouble with the rumor mill I think you just started."

"Okay, Rod. But first, settle one question I've always had. Was I the only female on base you didn't bed?"

"You and the African Queen." He tried to be glib, then turned redder. "Seriously, Rachel, there must have been two hundred women there. I couldn't possibly have slept with them all."

True, but not from lack of trying. Rod was wild and carefree back then—a nineteen-year-old, long-horned, Oklahoman stud fresh off the range—sniffing at anything that showed an interest. How he avoided court-martial or paternity was anyone's guess. "Hot Rod" did not refer to Rodney, Roderick or Rodecker. Not that I was any less randy—truth to tell—just more discreet. Many of those women he failed to entice were curled in with me.

Oh, and the African Queen. There's a sweet memory. Captain Helen Abernathy, the toughest, stracist MP commander any soldier would wish to follow. And I would have followed her to bed if she'd been bent the right way. She encouraged Rodecker to apply to OCS. She also convinced me, in a motherly and subtle way, that no matter how good a soldier and cop I wanted to be, the Army was not the best career choice at that time for someone of my persuasion.

There were a lot of us in uniform then, men and women, who were gay. I'm sure there are even more now. We were proud to serve, "to protect and defend the Constitution of the United States of America against all enemies." But Captain Abernathy was right. Even after "Don't Ask/Don't Tell" went into effect, it was too hard, at least for me, to live a lie and pretend I wasn't what I was—or too scared of getting caught.

Funny, I hadn't seen Abernathy or Rodecker in more than 10 years and they were both, now, successful civilian cops. Yet within the last six months, I had spoken with Helen looking for someone and here I was with Rod looking for another.

"The reason I'm here, Rod, I'm looking for a girl. No wise-ass remarks are necessary. She's a fourteen-year-old runaway her family wants found." I gave him two photographs from my shoulderbag."

"Missing Persons is down the hall."

"I know. I filed a report with them before coming in here. I'm hoping to spread the interest. The portrait is this year's school photo. The other was taken last summer. She's been missing three weeks."

Rod stared at the photos: a close-up of a blonde, freckled, serious-faced teenager and another full-length of the same girl in a bathing suit.

"Did you look like this at her age?"

"Same hair, same eyes, same bosom. Which is partly why I want to find her. I think she's ripe for exploitation. You know the kind I mean. The longer she's out there, the more dangerous life can be. Her family's worried and wants her home. I've been working it nearly a week but haven't found her yet on my side of the river, so I'm trying over here."

"What's her story?"

"Her name is Linda Miller; small town farm girl. Again, a lot like me. She started blooming in sixth grade. Her father had a hard time resisting what he saw and started sexually abusing her when she turned thirteen. I'm surprised he waited that long. It went on for months before anyone found out. The bastard's in prison now. The girl was in therapy and living with her mother and grandmother when she ran away. She thinks it's her fault *Her Daddy* went to jail. Last week she called a friend from the bus station. That's when the family hired me to find her and get her home. I'm hoping she's still somewhere in the area."

Rod focused on a picture on his desk of a nice looking woman and three young children. Two girls and a boy. Was there another Triple-R out there? Rod's expression said he'd like to kill someone. I would too, but I could only wish.

"Is this just a job or a personal quest?"

"The grandmother's ill. There are three younger daughters. The mother's hanging on the best she can. With *Daddy* in prison, the farm's suffering. I may charge them expenses, but I'll probably waive my fee. You saw her picture—she has the face of a young kid but is built like a brick you-know-what. What you don't understand is what she's endured: the teasing at school, the come-ons from older boys and men, the trauma of being a pedophile's victim. Yes, it's personal. I could easily have been her."

I left it there. I'd never been sexually abused, luckily, but I knew all about runaway. My last time was when I turned 18 and ran off to join the Army.

"I'll put the word out. See if we can get a lead on her. Can I keep these?"

"Sure, but I had these made to pass out."

I laid a packet of 4x6 photos from my bag on the table. Miller's school portrait was inset in one corner; the swimsuit shot filled the frame. On the back were personal details and contact numbers.

Rod looked at my card again. "Is your license any good here?"

What license? Another reason for lack of respect. My state doesn't require one and Rod wouldn't be overly impressed with my city-issued business license or my SAPI membership card. The State Association of Private Investigators has been lobbying for licensure for years to no avail. Maybe someday.

"No, but there's no law against a private citizen looking for someone or asking questions. I won't misrepresent myself on your turf, Rod. That's not how I do business. It's why I came to you. If I can find her, I will. If I need legal backup, I'll call you. I'm no Lone Ranger."

"Okay, Rachel. We'll help as long as you know the rules. I can't cut corners for old friends. I'll call as soon as I find out anything."

Two

MARGO LANE WAS a statuesque silhouette at the end of the aisle. Hand on hip, Margo spoke to several people on the lighted stage in the background.

"Ladies, please. We can do this. Let's try it again. Single line. Number three and number six please step forward. On toe. Pirouette. Again. Thank you. Step back."

"Excuse me,"

Margo turned. "The club's closed. We're conducting an audi . . . Whoa, Elsie! I think you have the wrong audition place, Honey. The Cadillac Club is twenty blocks west on Cutter."

The Cadillac Club was a T&A strip joint. The bigger the T the better was their business plan.

"I don't work with rubber women." I may hate my breasts, but I can't let them be insulted.

"Are you implying those are the natural you, Honey?"

"More natural than anything you've got swinging, Sweetheart!"

As I've said, I don't take crap from men; not even transvestites. I held out my card. "Phil sent me."

Margo Lane was long and sinuous. Great muscle tone without bulk and no fat. Not my type, but I bet the boys loved him. He wore a black silk teddy, skin-tight black jeans and heels. The heels made him longer, leaner. I stand five-nine in flats and it was a long reach to meet his eyes. The eyes were deep brown. The creases around them and at the edge of his lightly rouged lips were happy lines. Margo Lane either laughed a lot or was constantly amused by life.

He studied my card in the low light and apparently read my motto. His eyes crinkled and his lips curled. Constantly amused had my vote.

"Ooooh, I'll just bet you are."

It started with his drawn-out *"ooooh."* His voice dropped several registers to the basement—every word resonated—sending vibrations that plucked a string deep within me. The string must have been attached to my clit because I was suddenly wet. I couldn't breathe, my cheeks burned.

Talk about shocked and awed. I hadn't felt anything so intensely since . . . What the hell? This was beyond . . . Nothing—no one—ever hit me quite like this. Not even . . . Certainly never a voice. Shit! Definitely never a man. My expressions must have said everything, because Margo seemed equally wide-eyed shocked by my overreaction.

He recovered first. "You said Phil sent you?" Thank God, he said it in a normal tone.

"Yes . . . ahem. About the beatings," I squeaked trying to find my voice.

TWO HOURS BEFORE MEETING Margo Lane, I rushed into Phil's Tearoom. Traffic was slower than expected coming back from seeing Rodecker. The Big Ben mantel clock over the hearth chimed the half-hour as I walked up to the hostess. I'm rarely so exactly on time for an appointment. I prefer arriving early. I hate being late. It's part of the discipline the Army drilled into me.

Philadelphia Long's Tavern & English Tearoom are two establishments that fill the entire first floor of a four-story brick building on Cutter Avenue six blocks from the river in the heart of the South Ferry district. The Tavern is an English-style pub that fills the larger space.

The Tearoom is cozy with 12 lace-covered tables for four plus three sitting areas by the windows, at the back, and near the hearth. The east wall is filled with tall French windows and two sets of French doors leading onto a garden patio where more tables are set up. A large portrait of Queen Elizabeth II sits above the hearth. English landscapes and cottage paintings decorate cool blue-green walls.

Philadelphia Long, the owner, is an Anglophile. Every spring she makes a trip to London and comes back with a ton of stuff as well as many English, college-aged women she hires on one-year contracts. They get a year in America, and Phil gets real English atmosphere.

The hostess must have been one of this year's acquisitions. I hadn't seen her before. She had long chestnut colored hair done up in a French braid and was wearing tuxedo pants, a black vest, a frilly white blouse, and a cameo on a black ribbon choker. I liked what I saw.

"I'm Rachel Cord. Miss Long is expecting me."

"Yes, she said to show you right in."

The hostess' gaze lingered on my bosom a moment longer than necessary. I thought I caught a slight gleam in her hazel eyes, but that may have been wishful thinking. Some people I don't mind taking an interest in my breasts. If that seems a contradiction, then it's a contradiction. I'm still going to get them fixed.

She looked at my bare hands. "Do you wear a size six?"

I liked the sound of her accent but wasn't sure if it was from Chelsea or Devonshire.

"Eight, actually."

The hostess gave me a pair of fawn colored, two-button shortie gloves she took from the cabinet beside her. I didn't tell her I had a pair in my bag; at Phil's, ladies wear gloves. I was touched she made the effort to pick a pair to complement my sporty and lightweight set of alpaca jacket and trousers and a cream blouse. Think Kate Hepburn in *Pat and Mike*.

I followed her through the room to the first set of French doors. It was too early for high tea, but nearly all of the tables were occupied, as were two of the sitting areas. There were very few men, most likely tourists placating their wives; all looked uncomfortable and probably wished they were in the tavern next door. Most wore ugly ties Phil's supplies.

At the far end of the room a violinist and cellist played something by Chopin. At least I think it was Chopin. Behind them on the wall was a large black-draped oil portrait of the late Princess Diana. We went out onto the garden patio. It was a perfect spring day, the first we'd had in weeks, but only one table was occupied.

"Dahling," said Philadelphia as we approached. "Thank you so much for coming. Sarah, we will start with tea, please. I will ring when lunch should be served. Otherwise, no disturbances, please. Thank you."

I watched Sarah walk away.

"Luscious, isn't she? She isn't dating anyone, if someone wanted to ask her out."

I tore my eyes from Sarah. "A right tasty bit of crumpet I think is the expression. I saw the choker. Where is she from?"

"East Suffolk."

So much for my ear for English accents. The women Phil hires may be straight or gay. It doesn't matter to Phil. But she makes sure they understand the Tearoom's clientele. The cameo choker prevents embarrassing incidents. It identifies those with a like bent and who wouldn't mind being asked out. Otherwise, hands off; no exceptions. The lack of a choker didn't mean the woman wasn't gay. It simply meant she wasn't available for asking out. The Tearoom is a femme haven; a great place to meet someone or to bring a date. It was always my favorite place, but I hadn't been there in a long time. Sarah could make me wish to come back more often.

"Phil, you didn't ask me to lunch to discuss my love life, did you?"

"Of course not, Dahling. But you could use one, you know. How long has it been?"

I didn't like where her question was headed. "Why did you need to see me?"

Phil smiled at my evasion but didn't pursue it. "We can discuss that after the tea is served."

A waitress wheeled over a cart with teapot and cups and left. No choker.

"Shall I be Mother?" The question was rhetorical as Phil began pouring.

Phil speaks with an ersatz "veddy British" accent. She's from North Carolina where her parents had owned a high-end furniture manufacturing plant and she was their only heir. You'd have to go back to before the Revolution to find the English in her family tree. She's a handsome woman. She looks 50, but is really somewhere between 60 and 75. No one knows for sure, and she doesn't tell. No one knows for sure which way she's bent, either. Another secret Phil keeps to herself.

After sipping tea and exchanging pleasantries on the wonderfulness of the weather and the flowers blooming in her garden, Philadelphia finally came to the point.

"Rachel, I need to hire you. The police have been no help at all."

I waited for her to tell me the problem. She rarely called me Rachel. *Dahling* was her preferred usage.

"As you may or may not know, I own the Kathouse on River Drive. Over the past two months several of the girls who perform there have been beaten after leaving the premises. The police say it's a rash of gay bashing that will run its course. The police *claim* they have no leads. I can't believe that. I don't think they are trying very hard."

The Kathouse is Miss Kitty's Kathouse Kabaret; a song, dance, and comedy revue heavy on sexual innuendo and political satire. The *girls* are drag queens and transsexuals. They put on a popular show that brings in audiences, straight as well as gay, from all over the region. It's the type of place you expect to find in San Francisco or maybe New York, not here in the Heartland. I try to catch the act every couple of months or so, but it's another place I haven't been in awhile. I knew Phil owned a lot of property but hadn't known she owned the Kathouse. I hadn't heard about the beatings and couldn't recall the last time there had been *a rash of gay bashing*. Most of the relevant news of late was about same-sex marriage and its pending legalization in Massachusetts. Had that stirred things up?

"What do you want me to do?"

"Find out who's doing this. These attacks are frightening. The last girl is in the hospital. He may die."

"Who is he?"

"Oral Roberts. He was new at the club."

"Oral Roberts?" I felt my eyebrows lifting.

Philadelphia smiled. "I know. Isn't it simply delicious? Rachel, please, will you help us?"

"Phil, the police are better equipped to handle this kind of thing, and they don't like interference."

"But they aren't doing anything."

"I'll just be stumbling over the same information they already have. I don't want to waste your money."

"It's mine to waste."

Phil freshened our tea as she awaited my answer. I try to avoid butting in on police business and knew from past experience my efforts weren't always appreciated. Still, the only thing I had going was trying to find Linda Miller. I had done everything I could with that and was waiting for feedback; it was unlikely the case would pay for itself.

I average three full-pay clients a month. This isn't exactly a get rich line of work. Many of my clients are families looking for runaways like Linda Miller—though I don't always have such a personal interest—or they're wives trying to get trash on their husbands for a larger divorce settlement. Occasionally, a defense lawyer hires me to check out an alibi or witness. Once in a while, someone will want me to investigate a scam or embezzlement, or something more serious. It's a mixed bag: an hour here, an hour there, then a lot of time in-between waiting for information to flow back in. Nothing continuous, so when I can, I work several cases letting progress determine what I do when. Eventually the hours add up. The in-between I try to fill with process serving, skip tracing and routine background checks. Anything to keep the income flowing. After taxes, office lease, secretary service and expenses, I manage to cover everything else—like my condo mortgage, food, clothing, etc. Anything left over—if there is anything left over—goes into my boob fund. One of these days I'll unload my albatross.

"Phil, I charge $100 an hour with a ten hour minimum, no refunds, no guarantees. If I haven't found a solution, I'll give you an update report and you decide if you want me to continue or not. If I find out anything useful, it goes to the police. If that's acceptable, we have a deal."

Phil reached into a straw bag lying beside her. She pulled out three slim bundles of cash and laid them on the table.

"Here is $3,000. I don't expect refunds. Find these miscreants, Rachel, as soon as you can. Please. I don't want anyone else hurt."

I put the money in my jacket. "Will any of the victims talk to me?"

"Speak with Margo Lane, my manager at the Kathouse. Margo was the first one beaten. He will know with whom else you should speak."

MARGO TURNED THE AUDITIONS over to his assistant while he and I retreated to the end of the bar. He drew each of us a pint of beer, and we sat there not speaking for several minutes. Neither of us seemed anxious to explore what just happened. I still tingled from whatever it was his voice did to me. I had no idea what he was thinking. He refilled our glasses. I took out a notepad and pen.

"Tell me about the beatings."

My voice was back to normal and, fortunately, he kept his voice that way also. The first beating happened the Saturday night after Philadelphia left for London. At 2:45 a.m. Margo was the last to leave. The only vehicles in the lot were Margo's car and a refrigerator truck used to store extra beer for the weekends.

"I started across the lot to my car when four men appeared. They looked like college jocks dressed in warm-up suits. Maybe football players. Big. One came out of the shadows from across the lot. Another came from around the front of the club. The other two appeared from the shadows behind the reefer, surrounding me." Margo paused and took a deep breath before continuing.

"Someone yelled, 'Hey, faggot! We don't want your kind in our town.' Then they started hitting me. They only used their fists, but they hit hard." Margo paused again. "I broke loose and dove under the reefer. They couldn't get at me without crawling under the truck. A few kicks at their faces and they stopped trying. They shouted obscenities and more warnings, and then they left."

Margo didn't report the attack to the police.

"I didn't think it would do any good. It could have been worse. I had a swollen ear and some scrapes and bruises. A couple blows hit me hard in the kidneys. I peed pink part of the next day. Stayed home; didn't go to the hospital or come back here until we needed to open Tuesday."

Margo took a deep drink of his beer. "I didn't want to come back, you know. Those guys scared me. I've heard nasty comments before. We all have. That's nothing. Part of life. Even nasty things thrown at you, you can usually handle. This was different. I didn't know what to do."

14

They called the police after the second attack. The attacks were pretty similar: at or after closing, when few people were around; a single victim within three blocks of the club; and, at first, on a Friday or Saturday night. The assailants were four, white, college-age men with short hair wearing dark colored warm-up suits. They were big and muscular like bodybuilders or football linemen. They seemed to come from nowhere and then disappear. After the second attack, they began wearing ski masks. Whether or not they were the same men each time, no one was sure, but it was probable according to the police. The descriptions were too generalized for positive ID.

The police investigated each attack. They found no witnesses—except for the victims—nor did they find any evidence worth using, or so they said. After the third attack, increased police patrols made random passes of the area, especially around closing time. There were even a couple of stakeouts.

Then the attacks happened on other nights of the week. The ferocity increased also. The assailants began using sticks and bricks. Bones were broken. One performer was sodomized with a cut-off broomstick. The last attack, the one on Oral Roberts, happened last Thursday while the club was still open. Roberts had just walked out the front door when he was hit up side the head with probably a baseball bat and then thrown through the front window. It happened very quickly. Somehow, no one saw who did it. There was only the sound of a vehicle speeding away. Roberts was in a coma.

The club didn't open Friday or Saturday. Everyone was too upset. Too scared. No one went anywhere alone. Several performers quit. Some left town. Others found work at other clubs.

Margo was having a difficult time getting new performers, but he wanted to open a new revue.

"We can't close down. I can't let these attacks beat us."

"What are the other clubs doing?"

"I don't know. I don't think they've had any trouble."

Three

It WAS THREE in the morning. I had eaten every piece of food in my place that didn't require cooking. My bottle of Glenfiddich was two-thirds empty. I was agitated. Couldn't sleep. Couldn't think. As hard as I tried, I couldn't concentrate or make real sense of anything I learned that afternoon.

When I left the Kathouse, I stood outside for a moment looking at the plywood placed over the window Oral Roberts had been thrown through. There were two streetlights that would light the front of the building and sidewalk at night. Even at one in the morning, someone should have seen what happened. River Drive is a busy four-lane street along the river from one edge of the city to the other. It starts at North Ferry and runs south past Lincoln Heights. Beyond the city limits it's County Road 1.

I went around the side of the building to the parking lot where Margo was attacked. This was out of the way. It wasn't as well lit. There were places to hide. I could picture an attack happening here rather than out front. I made a note to tell Phil or Margo they should add lighting and some outside security cameras. I came back to the front of the building and looked across to Riverside Park.

Most of the nightlife in the area is clustered along Cutter Avenue. The Kathouse, on the other hand, has a wonderful location seven blocks north of Cutter overlooking the park and the river. The park starts three blocks north of Cutter beyond the wharves where the land begins to rise in low bluffs above the river. It's a narrow swath of green space between a hundred yards and two hundred yards wide and more than a mile long. There are places along it where you can climb down to the river to swim and fish. Private places where you could skinny-dip, if you dared, or have a quiet tryst with your girlfriend. The park's open with well-spaced trees, picnic areas and public restrooms. Parking is in a narrow lot running the length of the park and is separated from River Drive by a grassy divider strip with "In" and "Out" cutouts.

I walked across to the park. After talking with Margo, I spoke with George Dunn, the bartender and second victim. The second attack occurred in the park parking lot where George liked to leave his car. On busy nights, a lot of the club's customers parked there also. There were no lights in the parking lot. The only illumination would come from streetlights on the other side of River Drive. This area would have been ill lit at the time of the attack. Just like the attack on Margo.

I looked back at the Kathouse, a converted two-story warehouse that had kept its original exterior. Neon lights on the front of the building formed an outline of a giant green cat winking at the world. This had been an aging industrial area. Renewal began in the late eighties. The factories and warehouses south of the Kathouse had been renovated into offices, apartments and river view lofts. The city had built Riverside Park then. The building north of the Kathouse was another warehouse that had seen many uses over the years and was now closed up. A bold "SOLD" was pasted across a large "For Sale" sign.

I crossed back over River Drive and walked north past a moving and storage company, an auto parts store, a second-hand furniture store, and, incongruously, a deli and catering shop. Beyond that the factories and warehouses had been torn down. A large billboard announced a new condominium and townhouse community: "The Bluffs at Riverside, Phase I. *'Your dream come true'* for under $200,000. The Riverside Development Company." An eight-foot high, chain-link fence to keep out trespassers ringed the entire construction area.

The third attack happened at the corner by the deli a little after two in the morning. The victim had been grabbed, pulled down the side street into the dark, and then beaten. There were no street-level windows on the side of the building housing the deli, but maybe someone living upstairs had heard or seen something. Across the street was the construction site that would have been deserted that late. Maybe there was a night watchman I could interview. I was sure the police had asked around, but Margo claimed they had no clues. Once again, the attack had been out of the way, in the shadows — not like the attack on Roberts.

The attackers were getting bolder. They hadn't been caught. Maybe they were feeling invincible. What were their motives? They were going to make mistakes. I was sure the police thought so, too. The police were waiting for those mistakes; waiting for another attack. More attacks meant more chances for clues and more chances of catching the perpetrators. I didn't want that to happen: more attacks meant someone could die.

There were three more attack sites I should have gone to, but I was having trouble concentrating. Every time I tried to recall details of what Margo and George told me, I kept hearing Margo's *"ooooh."* A shiver knifed through me and I'd squeeze my legs together. I couldn't handle it, so I went straight home.

Margo had said something that bothered me — besides the sound of his voice, that is — but it eluded me all evening. I tried to think about Linda Miller but had no idea where that was going. Phil's personal questions vied for attention, but I easily avoided them. There were no new messages to look to for help. The TV offered no distraction. I couldn't concentrate, couldn't relax. Margo's *ooooh* kept taunting me.

Like many others, I'm sensitive to sound. A toddler's screeching or fingernails on a chalkboard often causes great pain. Whereas the low rhythm and beat of a bass fiddle or guitar, a Johnny Cash song, Elvis singing *In the Ghetto*, or James Earl Jones reciting a monologue on baseball brings warm sensations approaching ecstasy. Margo Lane took that sensation to a whole other level.

I took the hottest shower I could stand. Let the water blister me red as I turned round and round beneath the spray. Let the heat melt the tension, the tingling. Then I switched the spray to cold and stayed there till I was thoroughly chilled. It didn't help.

So I ate and drank and obsessed.

Now it was three in the morning. I was drunk enough to do what I rebelled against all evening. I punched in the phone number Margo gave me and held my cell phone to my ear. I didn't want him to answer yet I was dying to hear that voice again. I had to know if that afternoon experience was just a fluke.

"Hello?"

I couldn't say anything.

"Is anyone there? Who is this? What do you want?"

What should I say? Tell him why I called? Tell him I wanted to hear—

"Ooooh, it's you." His voice dropped down to that same low, tantalizing vibe.

The phone provided no buffer. It hit me again, just as it had at the Kathouse. It wasn't a fluke. I couldn't believe it. I was instantly wet. Every nerve ending twitched. I could barely breathe. My heart thumped like a jackhammer. I don't know if I made a sound or not.

"Is this a one-sided conversation?" His voice returned to normal and I held my breath. "I guess it is. You're not calling about the attacks, are you?"

No, I'm not. I couldn't speak out loud.

"You must be one sick bitch."

Yes, I am. I'd have to be to be doing this.

"Still not talking? I should hang up on you; you know that, don't you? There are more.... Aw, to hell with it. *I know what you want.*"

I squeezed my thighs together and bit my lip. Hoped he couldn't hear the moans welling within me. I wanted to hang up but couldn't. How did he know who this was? Caller ID, most likely. It didn't matter. It didn't matter as long as he kept speaking in that special way. And he kept speaking. I hated it. I loved it. I don't know how long he talked or what he said or how many orgasms wracked my psyche. I didn't care. I just wanted it to continue. In the end, I knew he could hear my fluttered breathing and the mewing sounds I made. It no longer mattered. I vaguely heard him say "Good night."

Four

I AWOKE SURPRISINGLY clear-headed. Surprising because I was at a complete loss to explain how or why what happened happened. I also knew how much I had had to drink. The nearly empty bottle was on the nightstand.

I had been totally possessed. I couldn't explain it. I certainly didn't understand it. My body still tingled from the rhythm and tone of his voice plucking my strings. This was crazy. A Man? Never! That bastard defiled me! No, wait. I called him. I did this to myself. I betrayed me, but why? This was crazy. It was nasty, dirty—but damn—I felt wonderful.

It was past noon; I should have been out already, getting information, searching. Instead, I wandered through my place lazily picking up chocolate wrappers, empty chip bags, banana peels, apple cores, an empty pint of *Cherry Garcia*, and the rest of the assorted debris from what I had consumed the night before.

I stopped at the bookcase; hesitated; felt the emptiness, the heartache. I picked up the picture that had lain face down in its frame for too many months. Dust outlined the shape of the frame clearly on the shelf. Karen stared at me with her impish smile. Longing filled me, overpowered me.

"I miss you so much."

My sight blurred. Tears streamed down my face. I wanted to hold her. Feel her body against mine again. Taste her raspberry lip balm. Hear *her* voice whispering into my ear not Margo's low vibrations. Feel her bubbling laughter as her tongue tickled me.

I wanted Karen—God! I wanted Karen—but she was gone.

"Eight months, Karen. Why? I love you. I thought you loved me. Where are you? Why won't you come home?"

I blinked her picture back into focus. Her dark, almond-shaped, sparkling eyes accentuated her Japanese heritage; her black silky hair blown back by wind from the river. Her smile that always seemed to say she had a secret.

"My sweet, gentle Sansei. It must have been my fault. I'm sorry. Please come home."

I placed Karen back on the shelf, as she should be, looking out on the world with unrepentant optimism. She was gone, but I could not deny how much a part of me she was. Deep down I knew I would have to accept her leaving, for whatever reasons she had, would have to try to live only with memories, but it hurt. The loss still hurt.

Maybe Phil was right. Maybe I did need a love life again. Maybe what happened with Margo was a catharsis, or something, I needed to break a shell I hadn't realized I built, reawakening feelings I had hidden. That had to be it. Maybe his voice was a fluke after all; something I could now deny and be cured of.

I STRODE INTO PHIL'S still in a Kate Hepburn mode. Casual tan trousers. Comfortable shoes. A man's white dress shirt with open collar and the cuffs rolled back above the wrist. A pale new-bud green sweater draped over my shoulders. My hair was cut way too short and my breasts were too large, but what the hell, I felt like Kate, anyway. I carried a pair of four-inch slip-ons in the same shade of green as the sweater.

Sarah wasn't there to greet me, which was a disappointment. I had hoped to see her again. Elspeth had the hostessing honors, and her soft burr of the Scottish highlands was as much a delight to the ear as she was to look at. I knew it was a Scot's burr because she had told me where she was from once before. She wasn't wearing a choker. Too bad.

The Tearoom wasn't as busy as the day before. As we walked through the room, several women looked interesting. I knew a couple of them casually, but had never dated them. Maybe I should. One woman, having lunch with I presumed her husband, watched me as I crossed the room. She fingered her chin like you might see a roué finger his beard and she smiled at me with a gleam in her eye. I smiled back. Did her husband know? Were they looking for a threesome? Not my style. Or was she just thinking of trying the better side? Hmmm. Margo's voice was awakening a lot of feelings.

Elspeth seated me on the garden patio. I asked if Miss Long were there and if she could join me. Elspeth went off to check. Phil lived on the top floor of the building.

I ordered a three-egg omelet with fresh asparagus and Gruyere, rye toast, the fruit of the day, and a pot of Earl Grey. The tea came first and I let it steep as the May sun warmed me. I suddenly realized I was thirty-three years old. I was so busy looking for Linda Miller yesterday—and then that thing with Margo—that I missed my birthday. Oh, well. Time flies, they say. So do birds. Several sparrows flitted about the patio looking for tidbits and crumbs. Bees hummed amidst the plethora of colors, textures, scents and life. Two yellow butterflies performed a swirling dance, each trying to get above the other—spinning, twisting, dancing, higher and higher, thirty, forty feet or more—till one broke away and they descended lazily back to the garden only to find each other again and begin their dance anew.

Honeysuckle and jasmine floated on the air mixed with juniper and rose. Within the maze of flora were hidden trysting places where couples could sip their tea in private intimacy or birds could seek grubs or worms or bathe in a shallow fountain. Beyond the hedges were the parking lot and Sixth Street.

When Phil was renovating this building for the Tavern & English Tearoom, what became the garden and parking lot had been two derelict buildings. One night both buildings burned. Phil bought the lots, cleared out the rubble and built her patio, garden and parking lot. Some said she paid to have the buildings torched. They may be right or not, I wouldn't know; I'm neither judge nor jury. I came across the story though while doing research on another matter. It was a large fire that nearly included neighboring buildings—including this one—before it was brought under control. It was ruled an accident: a homeless person trying to stay warm started the blaze. In July.

Phil joined me as I finished my omelet. She carried a cup and saucer and a pot of fresh tea. She sat down and poured for both of us.

"Dahling, you look like you swallowed a canary. Was it anyone I know?

My smile broadened into a Cheshire grin. "A lady never tells."

"Well, whomever it is, it's an improvement. You look better for it."

I didn't feel comfortable telling her what happened with Margo. I was still wrestling with that whole weird concept and it was defeating me. I was trying to ignore it. Still, I did feel better and I guess it showed. But that wasn't what I wanted to see Phil about.

"Phil, is anyone trying to buy the Kathouse?"

"Of course, Dahling. Developers are always making offers. But it is not for sale. It's the most profitable property I own. Why?"

"Just an idea I'm trying to work out. Has anyone been particularly persistent?"

"One or two, I would imagine. Does this have anything to do with the attacks?"

"It might. But I want to check a few things first. Could you get me the names?"

"Certainly. I will speak with my business advisor today. Will you tell me what you think it is?

"Not yet. Still too nebulous. I could be wrong. I'll let you know." I stood and picked up the lunch check.

Phil reached for it. "I will take care of that, Dahling."

"Don't be silly. I'm on an expense account. I have a rich client, you know."

I was still smiling when I walked out onto Cutter Avenue and headed west. A neatly dressed man with a clipboard stopped me.

"Excuse me. Are you a city voter?"

"Yes."

"We're petitioning to change the name of Cutter Avenue to South Ferry Avenue. South Ferry is—"

"I've already signed it. Twice, I think. Good luck."

Cutter Avenue was originally South Ferry Street, from the name of the community when ferries were the main way to cross the river. As the city enveloped the area, the name survived as both street and district. The street was renamed in the mid-1900s after some politician or war hero. Many locals want to change the name back as part of the current historical preservation kick; and, there is a North Ferry Avenue on the north side of the city where another ferry service once operated. But, actually, in a tongue-in-cheek way, the petition is an effort to recognize the gay community. There are more gay businesses concentrated along Cutter Avenue than anywhere else in the city.

Which is what had bothered me about what Margo had said. He said none of the other clubs had had any trouble. Why not? What about other gay-owned businesses? If this was a gay-bashing streak, it wasn't logical that only one gay business would be targeted.

Why the Kathouse?

This was what I wanted to check out. If the Kathouse were the only place targeted, then this probably wasn't gay bashing. It was a direct attempt to hurt the Kathouse. Which was why I wanted to know about any persistent buyers. This could be gay bashing. Or, it could be a personal vendetta: maybe a straight customer had been hit on or embarrassed and didn't like it; or someone was fired and wanted revenge. But I didn't think so. It didn't feel right; it had been going on too long. As Gene Vidoc taught me, "Follow the money. Whoever profits most likely did it."

I crossed Cutter to get to my bank on the corner at 12th Street before heading to the office. The JJ twins were coming out of the First State Bank & Trust.

"Where are you two going all dressed up?"

Janet Petrie and Janet Gentry were identically dressed in men's white dinner jackets, lilac dress shirts with black bow ties, black dress slacks and cummerbunds and black patent shoes. Each wore a rosebud boutonniere. One of them wore it on the left lapel. The other wore it on the right. They both had blue eyes and long straight blonde hair. One parted hers on the left, the other on the right. They looked like twins, although they weren't related, and always dressed as mirror images of each other. I never knew who was who.

"We're on our way to City Park," Janet started.

"To get married." The other Janet finished.

They always finished each other's sentences. They had been a couple for years longer than the four I had known them.

"I didn't know it was legal yet. When did we win?"

"It isn't," one started.

"And we haven't, yet." The other finished. "We're part of the national protest."

"For same-sex marriages. Fifty of us went down to the County Clerk this morning."

"To apply for marriage licenses. Of course we were refused."

"But it was fun watching them scramble around. We're all gathering downtown this afternoon in City Park."

"The South Ferry Faeries have a permit to throw a party in the park from four to ten. We don't think the city knows."

"It's going to be a wedding party. We have four Unitarian ministers."

"Who are going to conduct religious wedding services at sunset. Join us."

"And help us celebrate."

"Everyone will be there."

Janet and Janet are loads of fun, but you can hurt your neck swinging back and forth to follow their conversation. I usually just step back and look between them and let their images merge in the middle. I wished them happiness and said I would try and make it, but my schedule was pretty full. I watched them walk away hand-in-hand.

Would Karen and I have married had it been legal? Would she have run away if we had?

After depositing most of Phil's money, I walked south to where 12th Street ends at Mann Avenue and the Mann Avenue Plaza. The plaza is an old U-shaped high school building fitted around a large courtyard and redeveloped into offices in 1990. I moved in in '98 when I started my agency. If you can call a one-woman operation an agency. I don't know what else to call it. I've never heard a detective business called anything else. My office is on the second floor of the west wing.

At the top of the stairs, Doris Garrity was in the round reception center in the hall. Doris and Mary Farr provide secretarial services to many of the small businesses on the second floor.

"Hi, Rachel. You're getting a late start. I have two messages and here's your mail."

"Long night. Thanks Doris." I read the messages as I walked down the hall.

On one she had written, "P. Jays called. Has info you wanted." PJs is a grandmother who runs an unofficial center for displaced youth out of her two-story home. There's a home in every neighborhood that just seems to draw young people to it. Mrs. McComber's was where I remember practically living at as a teenager. That's PJs' place. It's been that way for more than 40 years, she says. Ever since her own children started walking and brought friends home. Nowadays nearly every runaway in the city seems to gravitate to PJs, just as I always headed for Mrs. McComber's. I hoped the message was good news about Linda Miller.

The other message was from Frank Taylor. "Turn your cell on or check your voice mail." His message made me realize my cell phone still lay on the bed. A flash memory of Margo's voice twanged me.

Frank is a police detective in the South Ferry District I've known for six years, ever since I started this business. We met on a case. He's my other best contact and a good friend. His message could be about Linda Miller also. But Frank's messages often bring bad news.

My office is half of an old classroom. These old rooms had two entrances. To make affordable office space, the developers split many of the larger classrooms in two by adding two large closets. One for each office. The room was still large and the tall windows make it light and airy. I keep the schoolroom look. My desk is an old oak teacher's one from the 1930's that sits in front of the blackboard. I have two rows of three tables where I spread out the cases I'm working. I use the blackboard to work out problems. There are two loveseats set by the near window corner where I interview clients.

I tossed the mail on my desk—there was nothing interesting except the latest issue of *PI Magazine*—and called Frank. If he had bad news, I wanted to get it over with.

"Taylor here."

"It's Rachel. You've been trying to reach me?"

"I got a lead on your lost runaway. I'm on my way to lunch. Join me and I'll fill you in."

"Okay. I'll be there in twenty minutes."

At least he didn't say they had found a body. I called PJs.

"City Morgue. You stab 'em, we slab 'em."

"Let me speak with PJs, please."

"Just a mo."

"This is PJs, how may I help you?"

"This is Rachel. Who's the comic answering the phone?"

"That was Erica. I hope she wasn't offensive."

"Not at all. I got your message."

"It's about the girl you're trying to find. Two of the girls staying here saw her last week."

"Do they know where she is?"

"They might, but they're being cautious. They don't want to get her into trouble. They're afraid you may be from the police or Social Services. It would be best if you spoke to them directly."

"Are they there now?"

"No, but they will be here for dinner. This is meatball and spaghetti night if you would care to join us. We eat at five o'clock."

"Thanks, but I'm having a late lunch so I don't think I'll be hungry. Would it be all right if I came by between five-thirty and six?"

"That will be fine, dear. I do hope you find the poor girl."

"I'll try. Thanks again. Bye."

Two leads on Linda Miller. Things were looking up. I told Doris I wouldn't be back and went to meet Frank for lunch. Lunch with Frank Taylor means Charlie's Chicago Hot Dog Stand. I didn't need to eat again so soon, but when you lunch with Frank, you better eat lunch. He doesn't understand how anyone could pass up any chance at eating an authentic Chicago hot dog.

Five

FRANK SAT AT ONE of the picnic tables in the shade of a large spreading oak. It's a surprise no one's ever cut it down and put an office building on that corner. Charlie's is a small white building with half a dozen parking spots. There are some counter spaces inside if the weather is bad, but most people order from the window and sit under the tree.

Frank was contentedly chewing and holding half a hot dog. Another one waited on the platter in front of him. Frank's a big brown bear. He looks soft, but there's taut muscle underneath. His skin is polished chocolate and gray salts his short kinky hair. Frank transferred here from Chicago about 15 years ago because of illness in his wife's family. He wants to put in another five years before retiring, hopefully, back to Chicago. A die-hard fan of both the Cubs and the Sox, he still misses going to home games. His one pleasure is his daily hot dog fix.

"Hi, Rachel. Charlie said he'd fix yours as soon as you got here. It's paid for."

The classic Chicago hot dog is a work of art, and Charlie's version is no exception. A huge all-beef hot dog nestled in a toasted poppy-seed bun and covered with yellow mustard, onions, chopped cucumber, tomato wedges, neon green relish, Greek peppers and celery salt. Hot dog and salad all in one. Charlie serves it with a dill pickle spear, or with fries or slaw and a drink. Charlie also serves a slaw dog and a chilidog, and chili fries or a bowl of chili, but that's it.

Don't ask for ketchup for the fries, because Charlie doesn't have any. He's afraid you may put it on the hot dog and will give you a five-minute lecture on such blasphemy.

Frank started on his second hot dog as I took my first bite.

"A guy was picked up last night peddling kid pix at the Cadillac Club. This morning, I found your girl in one of them."

I stopped eating. I didn't want to ask.

"It was tame. Just a bikini shot showing off her breasts and young, but pouty, face. Not as bad as some of the others."

"Who's the guy? Was he the photographer? Does he know where she is?"

"Just a smut peddler. Won't give us his source yet. We're trying to convince him and his lawyer that cooperation is in his best interest. All we have so far is he bought the pix across the river."

Across the river. Glad I went to see Rodecker. I'd let him know about the photos.

"Speaking of across the river, I'm hearing tales about you and 'Hot Rod' Rodecker."

Frank smiled and took another bite of hot dog. I'm not sure what my face looked like, but he seemed to find it amusing.

"Come on, Rachel. Don't you think we cops talk to each other? You probably weren't back before I had a call wanting to know who you were."

"What did you say?"

"Just the truth. That you're a private dick that plays fair and knows her place. That's a stretch, I know, but, hey, we're friends. They were hoping you were Rodecker's secret mistress."

"His what?"

"Mistress. Rodecker came in there as a hotshot a few years ago and the brass just promoted him to captain over many senior people. That's why they call him 'Hot Rod.' Figure he's racing for the top spot in record time. He's too young and jumped to the head of the line. He's stepped on toes, so someone wants to rein him in with a little leverage."

Damn. That explains those looks I got.

"Frank, when you talk to them again, tell them Rod and I were both MPs during the Gulf War. I went to see him strictly in connection with trying to find Linda Miller."

"No problem. I want to call them this afternoon, anyway. See if they know who the photo source could be. If she's over there, they'll find her. It's good you brought them into it."

If Frank were going to call, I wouldn't need to. Rod didn't need to hear from me so soon under the circumstances, and, hopefully, the rumors would quiet down.

"One other thing, Frank. Do you know anything about the beatings at Miss Kitty's Kathouse Kabaret?"

"Not a lot. That's Ed Montero's case. I know he's pissed about it. It's been going on for a couple of months and he hasn't made any progress. What's your interest?"

"The Kathouse people are pissed there's been no progress, so they hired me to look into it. Any idea what Montero's problem is?"

"Ed's no homophobe, if that's what you're thinking. He's pissed he hasn't caught these guys and that the brass are playing the thing down. It's low priority. The official stance is that it's an isolated temporary thing. There's only Ed, his partner, and two beat officers working it. But that could change if the guy in the hospital dies. But you better be careful about interfering in an ongoing investigation."

"I will. Have there been other gay bashing incidents?"

Frank chewed on his hot dog as he gave the question some thought.

"We get fights and muggings and such all the time. But nothing I'd call gay bashing. Just these beatings. Seems kinda strange, don't you think?"

"Yes, I do."

THE CADILLAC CLUB WAS only a few blocks from Charlie's. It was a little after four; I had time before I needed to be at PJs. I wanted to know if anyone there could give me a lead they hadn't passed on to the police.

On my way there, I had to pass Brownie's, a gay country dance club. Jeremiah T. Browne, the owner, was outside leaning back in a chair with his eyes closed. His ever-present weathered Stetson cocked back so the sun shone on his face.

"Hey, Brownie. What are you doing out here?"

"Workin' on my tan, Big Mama. What did you think?"

Ask a stupid question. Tan would not have made my first ten guesses. Brownie has dusky blue-black tones evoking images of deepest Africa. His place is decorated with the images and gear of Black cowboys like Bill Pickett and the 9th and 10th Cavalries. If you let him, he'll bend your ear all night with stories of how the Black Man helped build the West. Which is a good way to learn some history. When Brownie's storytising, the beer's free.

"Have you heard about the beatings over at the Kathouse?"

Brownie sat up. "They're a terrible thing, Rachel. Good people are gettin' hurt. I hope they catch those bastards."

"Have you had any problems?"

"Nah. Everything's quiet around here. Seems like it's jest the Kathouse those assholes are messing with. Are you looking into it, too?"

"I'm trying. The owner doesn't think the police are doing enough."

"Yeah, the police do what they can, but sometimes that doesn't cut it. If you find out who it is, I know some Buffalo

Soldier reenacters who would be happy to form a firing squad."

"Thanks. I'll keep that in mind. Don't get a sunburn."

"Never fear, Big Mama. Never fear."

I left Brownie soaking up the rays and went on to the Cadillac Club. The guy inside the door said, "There's a five dollar cover."

"I'm not here to see the show. Is the owner here?"

He stared at my bosom. "No, but the manager's at the end of the bar having dinner. He just hired some girls, but I'm sure he'll hire you. Go on in."

I left him with his misconception. Two young women on the stage in nothing but G-strings were doing sensuous bumps and grinds to a slow jazz piece. A couple dozen men watched and sipped beer, trying to make their two-drink minimum last. About half of them were wearing nametags for a local convention.

The guy at the end of the bar was working on a steak and baked potato. He was at least sixty and going bald. He looked at me when I stood beside him. "If you're looking for work, you can start tonight."

"I've got a job, and you can't afford me." I handed him my card. "I'm a private investigator and I'm here about the kiddie porn guy last night."

He didn't look at my card, but flipped it onto the bar and resumed cutting his steak. "Talk to our lawyer. We got nothing to do with that guy. If we'd known what he was doing, we'd have taken him to the river and tossed him in." He took a bite.

"Sure. I know you wouldn't condone that kind of trade in your place." Not unless you were getting a cut, that is. "I'm not with the police. What I hear stays with me. I'm looking for one of the kids in the photos he was selling. She's a runaway and her family is worried for her. I'm trying to get a lead on the photographer. Find out where the girl is."

"Can't help you," he said and stuffed a hunk of steak in his mouth.

I pulled out Linda's picture. "This is her. She's only fourteen."

He was wearing a wedding ring, so I took a final shot. "You have any daughters?"

He put down the knife and fork. "Yeah. Two. That's them on the stage right now. Working their way through college."

He wiped his mouth and continued. "I know what you're thinking, but you're wrong. I said we don't peddle that shit and I meant it." He paused and kind of sighed. "But you're right, I wouldn't want that crap to happen to one of my girls, or anyone else's. Talk to Carl at Triple-X Video over on Thirtieth. I hear he's not too particular about the stuff people bring him. But you didn't hear it here."

He turned back to his steak, but his appetite seemed to have waned. He sat there with a disgusted look. On my way out, I stopped for another look at the two girls on the stage. They were between eighteen and twenty and could be sisters. It was only late afternoon but they each had lots of bills sticking out of their G-strings.

Bob with the Regional Air Traffic Controllers Convention got up from a crowded table and stumbled my way. I knew all about him because that's what it said on the label pasted on a loud sports coat any car salesman would envy. He had had a bit more than the two-drink minimum.

"Wow! You got BIG honkers. Honk! Honk!" He squeezed my breasts.

I quickly squeezed his crotch—hard. His face paled and his eyes widened. No sound came from his gaping mouth.

"Thanks, Bob." I squeezed again. "And you got BIG cajones."

I ARRIVED AT PJS AT 5:45 after going back to my condo to get my cell phone and car. I could have walked, but I wanted to make it to J and J's wedding if possible.

The house was large on a street of large, privately owned homes south of Martin Luther King, Jr. Avenue in Lincoln Heights. PJs and her husband, Horace Johnson, had bought it after their third of six children was born. They had owned a successful liquor and convenience store at the corner of 13th Street and Division Avenue. Division is now Martin Luther King, Jr. Avenue.

Business and life had been good for them. Until the night Horace was killed during a robbery attempt at their store. He had a gun and was aiming it at the two thieves when the police arrived. The police officers didn't know him, thought he was the robber and shot him without warning. The police officers were white. The thieves were white. Horace was black.

PJs went into a long period of deep depression. Her children, neighbors, and the long string of young people who kept coming to her house eventually brought her out of it. During her depression she started wearing nothing but her husband's pajamas. Day or night, it didn't matter. When she recovered, she decided pajamas were the most comfortable clothing anyone would want to wear. So she went on wearing them. All styles, all colors, all kinds of material. Everywhere she went. That, and fuzzy slippers. She became the fashion queen of pajamas. That's how she got her name.

The tragedy of Horace's death caused two weeks of riots when the shooting was ruled an accident. The city finally made a large settlement. The settlement paid off mortgages on the house and store. Put her children and now her grandchildren through college. Let her provide a small annual scholarship to underprivileged young people. Let her run her home as a haven for any youngster who needed love, attention, or just a place to crash for the night.

As far as the city is concerned, PJs home is neutral territory. Police and Social Services go there only when invited. Her husband's death was long ago, but the neighborhood has a longer memory.

I went up the steps and in the ever-open doorway and stood in the hall. Sounds of clattering dishes, laughter, talk and music came from everywhere. The dining room on my left had a dozen people seated and eating happily. In the living room to my right, card tables had been pushed together and another group was eating there.

PJs oldest daughter, Ruth, came down the hall from the kitchen carrying a huge bowl filled with more spaghetti, meatballs and sauce. Ruth is a large breasted, big-hipped woman like her mother with the same rich mahogany skin. When I'm around Ruth and PJs I'm less self-conscious of my breasts. "You don't need to worry about your breasts, girl," Ruth would often tell me. "Just add some to your hips to balance them."

"Hey, Rachel. Mama's in the kitchen. Grab a plate and join us."

"Thanks, Ruth."

In the kitchen, three small children in highchairs were covered in sauce and slurping spaghetti. Another four children were eating at the table. The fragrance of oregano, garlic and hot grease filled the room. PJs supervised a youngster at the stove who was browning meatballs in a skillet. PJs wore an apron over a pair of Chinese red silk pajamas decorated with birds and cherry blossoms. Her fuzzy slippers were a matching red. I took a few black olives from a relish tray on the counter and waited.

Ruth came into the kitchen. "Mama, Rachel's here to see you."

"Oh, Rachel, honey. Thank you for coming. Are you hungry?"

"No thanks. I just had lunch."

"Ruth, dear, would you please take over here? Rachel and I have some things to discuss."

PJs and I went out into the hall.

"The two girls I told you about should still be in the living room. I'll get them and we can go upstairs where it's quieter."

PJs came back with two teenaged girls. The younger one was barely thirteen. She was fair-haired and fair-skinned and was wearing jeans and a T-shirt for a band called the *Flat Truants*. There were spots of sauce on the shirt. The other one was probably fifteen, but looked twenty-one. Her hair was dyed ink black and her makeup was overdone, heavy purple eye shadow and purple lips. She wore a low-cut red sheath that barely passed her crotch, and red heels but no pantyhose. Her outfit screamed "Hey! Look at me! I'm a stereotype! Don't I shock you?"

PJs said, "This is Barbara. This is Jennifer. Girls, this is Rachel Cord. The private detective I told you about who is trying to find your friend."

I handed each of the girls one of my cards. The younger one, Jennifer, giggled when she read it.

"Are you really?"

"When I have to be."

PJs led us upstairs to her sitting room. The girls sat on the loveseat. PJs sat in her rocker and I took the overstuffed chair.

"PJs tells me you may know where I can find Linda Miller. Is this her?"

I passed them one of the pictures I had of Linda. I wanted to be sure they weren't mistaken about whom we were discussing. Jennifer looked at the picture and back at me.

"Are you and she related?"

"No, we're not. Her family hired me to find her. They're very worried about her."

I understood Jennifer's question. Linda could have been a younger sister. My hair has turned browner over the years than Linda's blonde, and the freckles have all but disappeared, but the blue eyes are the same, and the bulging bosom completes the family picture.

Barbara was leaning back and biting the purple-painted nail of her thumb. "She's not going to get into any trouble, is she?"

"I think she may already be in trouble. The police arrested a man for selling pornographic pictures of children. Linda posed for some of them. If I can't find her, who knows what could happen to her."

They looked at each other. Jennifer nodded to Barbara.

"We were at this party last week," Barbara said. "That's where we met her. She said she was new in town. She came with some people she met at the bus station. We told her about PJs, but she went off with some photographer. That's the last we saw of her."

"Where was the party held?"

"A big house on the north side by the river. Close to North Ferry. It's a pretty ritzy place."

"It is so cool," Jennifer added. "It's like a mansion and there's this huge lawn that goes down to a dock on the river. There are two cool speedboats there. But I like the gazebo at the end of the dock best. I think it's romantic."

"Do you remember what night the party was?"

Barbara looked thoughtful. "I think it was Saturday. Not this last one, but the one before."

Jennifer shook her head. "No it wasn't. It was just last Wednesday. We were with Sheila. She drove."

"That's right. Wednesday. Not yesterday, but last week. Sorry. Sometimes it's hard to remember which party is which. Carl has parties there all the time."

"Who's Carl?"

"The rich guy that owns the place. He says kids should have a good time. Carl says there aren't enough party places. He's right, you know. This town's a drag."

"Do you know Carl's last name?"

"No. Just Carl."

"How did you know the guy Linda went with was a photographer?"

"He's always there taking pictures and he was trying to hire a bunch of us as 'fashion models.'"

"He offered us fifty dollars each," said Jennifer.

"Yeah, but he was really coming on to Linda. He was telling her 'You are so beautiful . . . a natural model' and things like that. It was just a line. I mean, you could tell she was just a kid with big tits. Sorry, no offence. I heard him offer her two hundred dollars. He said he could get her a job modeling. She left with him."

"Do you remember his name?"

"Calvin. I remember 'cause I asked him if he was Calvin Klein."

The girls gave me a few more details about the parties at Carl's and offered to show me where it was the next day. I thanked them for their help and gave them each $20. They were surprised. They weren't expecting money. They gave the money to PJs for the house food fund; maybe there's hope for today's youth after all.

I added my own contribution to the fund and thanked PJs for all of her help. She didn't really need the money, but she understood it was good to let people give.

As I left PJs, I wanted to call Rodecker about the photographer named Calvin. Maybe it would help Rod find the guy. However, I was still leery of fanning the rumors about Rod and me. I called Frank instead and asked him to pass the info along. I didn't tell him about the sex shop or the party house.

Were sex-shop Carl and rich Carl who throws parties the same guy or was it only a coincidence? I never put much stock in coincidence. I'd have to check it out, but first, there was a wedding to attend.

Six

THE WEDDING PARTY at City Park was going strong. The mood was giddy and light. Several hundred people sang and danced. Vendors passed out free food and soft drinks. A rainbow of balloons floated over the park's central fountain. Even the sky celebrated with blue and pink and purple and gold as sunset neared.

The park is one block square across from City Hall. It was cordoned with rainbow streamers to limit access to the paved entrances at each corner and center of each street. Streamers were tied to most of the trees. Some rent-a-cops— off duty police and sheriff's deputies—wandered about the perimeter.

In front of City Hall, a couple dozen protesters shouted and waved signs with typical slogans like "Homosexuality is a Sin," "Marriage = Man + Woman," "Gays Will Go To Hell," "Remember Sodom & Gomorrah," "Gays Aren't GAY!!!" Police officers kept them on the sidewalk. Once inside the park, the party drowned them out.

There were dozens of people I knew well. Scores I recognized. And hundreds I had never seen before. All of us brought together at this time and place to celebrate an event as old as society. I found J and J and wished them good luck again. I wished again Karen were there, that we'd find each other, but knew it wasn't going to happen. Instead I let the joy of the moment, and that of my fellow sisters and brothers, fill me, quell the pang and ache of emptiness, and carry me along.

As the sun went down, all of the couples and the ministers gathered in the center of the park—walking right into the shallow pool of the fountain where children splashed in the summertime. There were matching tuxedos and matching wedding dresses. There were Earth mothers garlanded with flowers. There was a young Adonis and a young Apollo: two bronzed gods in tunics and laurel wreaths. The rest of us formed three large rings around them, our arms linked. Three rings of unity. Three rings of love. Three rings of defense should anyone try to stop this wondrous moment.

The ceremonies were brief, filled with magic and pride. I watched two crones jump a broom with a splash; the two gods share a cup; J and J sing a paean of love to one another.

This was jubilation. Celebration. We swayed to music like ocean waves or vast prairie grasses moved by the wind. We laughed. We cried. We sang. We sang of love. We sang of joy. We sang of freedom. We sang our American dream.

I was euphoric: filled with rapture, delight; giddy with joy, cheer, elation; merry, blissful, lighthearted, zany. Hell! I was totally, wonderfully gay.

Then I saw Sarah. She was with Elspeth and others from Phil's. The weddings made them bubbly.

"Rachel," Elspeth said, rolling the R. "Wasn't that fantastic. I feel so grand. Do you know Eloise and Iris? And this is Sarah. Sarah just started this week at the Tearoom."

"Hi, everyone. Yes, I met Sarah yesterday."

On my birthday. Sarah's eyes sparkled and the confetti in her hair glittered.

"I'm happy to see you again," she said.

The others were talking and going on about the weddings, yet all I heard over and over was "I'm happy to see you again." The joy of the evening filled me, but those six words sent me to heaven. I was ever so happy to see her too.

Somehow we wandered away from the others. There were people and sounds and happenings all around us, but we floated in a bubble of our own making.

She wore her hair down and it caressed her bare neck and shoulders. We shared a funnel cake from one of the booths. I brushed powdered sugar from her cheek. She fed me a piece of the cake. We touched in a dozen subtle, sensual ways. I was quivering inside. Did she sense it?

We were high on the night's experiences. I wanted to stay; chat with her, spend time with her, get to know her better, tell her about me. I wanted to continue the rapport—the feelings—we were building, but I couldn't stay. I needed to check out the Triple-X Video Arcade. I needed to find something to lead me to Linda Miller.

"I don't want you to go."

"I don't want to go. I'd rather stay here with you. I . . . I have to work."

"Could we meet later?"

"I'd like that. Very much. Where?"

"There's a wedding reception later at Miss Kitty's cabaret. It'll probably last all night. Do you know it?"

"I do. I'll see you there as soon as I can."

"I'll wait for you."

I wanted to kiss her right then. Hold her tightly, passionately. Never let her go. I thought she might want that too. But we were shy, nervous, anticipatory. Like two teens on a first date. She squeezed my hand and smiled.

Seven

THE TRIPLE-X VIDEO ARCADE was in a strip mall facing 30th Street a few blocks north of Cutter and just outside of the South Ferry district. Strip mall fit: there was a strip joint, two XXX-video places and a bar & grill. A Christian Science Reading Room on one corner provided the only class. The parking lot was about half full.

Several men were studying video boxes as I entered. As usual, my leading elements captured everyone's attention. I ignored the adulation and walked up to the guy behind the counter.

"Are you Carl?"

"No, I'm Rudy. Carl doesn't work nights," he said to my chest.

"Do you know how I can reach him?"

"It's a party night, so he's at his house." He still spoke to my chest. "Were you supposed to meet him?"

I picked up on his error and lied. "Yes. I thought we were meeting here. I'm new in town and running very late. I don't know the address. I'd hate to get lost."

I gave him a big smile, not that he noticed.

"It's out by the river. 8715 North River Drive. That's the river side of the street."

"Thanks, Rudy. I'll find it. I'll tell Carl how helpful you were."

"Yeah. Have a good time." Rudy's gaze never shifted.

I wished all my interviews were that easy. I wanted to meet Sarah, but I couldn't pass up this opportunity. Barbara and Jennifer hadn't mentioned a party tonight, but there couldn't be two Carls having parties on North River Drive. I hoped Sarah would wait for me. I drove back to my condo to change clothes. I thought something like Barbara's look might be more appropriate.

NORTH RIVER DRIVE IS ONE of the ritzier neighborhoods, and along this stretch, individual addresses are easily a quarter mile apart. You can't see the river along here because of the walls, hedges and shrubs the owners use to insure their privacy.

I found 8715 and turned into the drive. There was a closed gate and a guard. The guard had a clipboard and walked over to my car. I lowered the window and took a deep breath. The spaghetti straps of my low cut sheath strained and added to the "I may pop out of my dress" look.

"Ah am lookin' for a party."

The guard grinned from ear to ear. "I think you've found it. Follow the drive down to the main house and someone will park your car."

"Why thank you so much."

He opened the gate with a remote control. It was a winding drive. Jennifer was right; it was a mansion. I counted 18 windows on the second floor and saw balconies at both ends of the red-brick house. All the lights seemed to be on. I heard music before I reached the house. Beyond, a broad lawn led to the river. I could just make out the gazebo Jennifer liked so well silhouetted against the water.

I waited a moment adjusting my dress and my Marilyn Monroe styled platinum wig and watched the valet park my car. The dress was longer than Barbara's, but not by much. I checked the numbered tag the valet gave me against its place on a pegboard filled with keys. If I needed to leave in a hurry, I didn't want to waste time searching for keys or car. There must have been a hundred vehicles packed together in a makeshift lot.

Hopefully, Calvin was here and I'd get the chance to go off with the bastard. It was remotely possible Linda Miller was here too. I didn't expect it. Life rarely cooperates that easily.

This was my second party of the night and they were worlds apart. Competing noise assaulted me as I entered. I should have brought earplugs. This wasn't celebration. This was frantic survival.

Punk rock blasted from a darkened room to my left. Across the infield-sized entry, I felt the beat and cadence of hip-hop coming full tilt from another darkened room. Strains of country rock filtered down from the second floor. Something for everyone. Strobe lights flashed above the heads of people crowding the music rooms' entries. People were everywhere. Young people. Kids. Why weren't they home studying instead of here? Sitting on the stairs. Flopped on chairs and couches or on the floor against a wall. Coming and going. Drinking canned sodas, bottled water, beer in plastic cups, or red-colored concoctions in plastic margarita glasses. The average age seemed to be sixteen, and there were many who were definitely younger. I felt old and didn't like it. Jeans and T-shirts prevailed, but there was some of everything. Two pale girls who could have been twins of Barbara slinked by and gave me the eye. They were too young for my tastes. A cradle robber I'm not. Hairstyles ranged from pixie to outlandish in every color from a 64-piece box of crayons.

A man nearer my age sauntered toward me doing a Hugh Hefner impression. He wore a chocolate lamé smoking jacket and gold chains around his neck. All he needed was the pipe. He seemed as out of time and place as I did. I doubted the young people here would be attracted to him. I certainly wasn't. Maybe Margo would go for him.

"Hello there. Welcome to the party. I know I've never seen you here before."

He had to speak loudly over the noise and it ruined the affect he was trying for. Also, his musky cologne was much too heavy.

"No, suh. You certainly have not. This is my first party since leaving Biloxi. I'm Charlotte. Are you my host?"

I extended my hand palm down and he actually kissed it. I don't know why I do it, but whenever I put on this type of outfit I become a sweet molasses-tongued coquette from the Deep South. Over the years, my "Shaaaa-let from Bi-loooxi" has gotten a rise from many suspected philanderers for my divorce-seeking clients. It's only playacting to verify the wanderers, but I always feel a double tinge of guilt when I do it. Not because I'm putting on some sleazeball guy, but because I'm self-exploiting my deformities and because I knew a Charlotte from Biloxi in the Army. Charlotte Grey. A sweeter lady you could never hope to meet. She was small, petite. Charming, but, unfortunately, not bent the right way. She certainly wasn't a coquettish sex kitten. But it's her voice that comes out when I do my act. Sorry, Charlotte.

He continued to hold my hand. "Regrettably, no. Carl's upstairs at the moment. I'm John, and I would be delighted to give you a tour, Miss Charlotte."

"You are just too kind, sir. Might a lady acquire a drink to carry along the way?"

"She may. Right this way."

A double staircase created a horseshoe arch to the second floor. John offered his arm and led me through the archway beneath the stairs into a large banquet room with a panoramic view of the river. I had a flash image of the two of us and wanted to laugh. All I needed was a pair of ears and a cottontail.

Buffet tables were set up along the windows and people were helping themselves. The food was mostly a variety of pizzas, boneless chicken strips and bags of popcorn. No veggies except for the mushrooms and green peppers on the pizzas. There were trays of iced canned sodas and bottled water. Most of the activity was at the bar at the end of the room. Beer and strawberry margaritas were being passed to anyone who wanted one. The three bartenders were asking everyone if they were over twenty-one, but weren't turning anyone away or checking ID. Naturally, everyone was saying yes.

John brought me a margarita. I took a small sip. It was sweet and on the weak side.

"Aren't you afraid of the police with all this underage drinking."

John shrugged. "Not a problem. They're just having fun. Let me show you around."

Fun?

The kitchen was stacked with pizza boxes from several delivery places and boxes of chicken. Two servants were filling trays and placing them in heating ovens. Someone removed a bag of popcorn from a microwave and started another bag popping. We went through a billiard room and peeked into a crowded home theater. What I thought might be an old copy of *Debbie does Dallas* was playing on a 60-inch rear-projection TV. There was a scent of incense mixed with sweet marijuana and sweat. Someone yelled, "Shut the door. You're letting the light in."

We went out a side door to the patio. The sound level dropped to where you didn't have to scream to be heard. There was a heated pool where several young people were swimming. I couldn't tell if they wore suits or not.

"Would you care for a swim?" John asked.

"I do not believe those youngstahs would care for an ole lady like me interfering in their fun."

"You're hardly old. It would do them good to see a real woman."

"You are just *so* sweet." Gag. "Perhaps another time."

"I look forward to it."

Never in this lifetime, buddy. The patio ran around the back and went the length of the house with entrances to the kitchen, banquet room and a living room with fireplace. A second story balcony from which I could hear country music covered part of the patio.

We passed a girl lying on a chaise who appeared to be unconscious. She looked sixteen or seventeen. She lay there like a discarded Barbie doll. Her lipstick was smeared. Someone had tried to redress her. Her skirt was twisted and her blouse misbuttoned.

"Is she all right?"

"I'm sure she is, but I'll get someone to look at her. I'll be right back."

I put my nearly full drink down. The girl's pulse was strong and her breathing normal. There was no smell of alcohol or marijuana. Her pupils were pinpricks. I didn't know what she had taken, but whatever it was, she was out for the night. A glimpse under her skirt confirmed she wasn't wearing panties. I looked in the purse that lay beside her. Her driver's license said she was Kayla Barnes and she was nineteen. Hard to believe. She lived at 6044 N. 128th Street, Apt. 2B. I read the address several times to memorize it. There was also a current student ID from Cramer College. There weren't any pills or packets of drugs. I put the purse back and stepped away as John returned with a tall lanky woman and two men.

"Charlotte, this is Gwen Archer. She'll take care of the girl."

"Should we call a doctor? She doesn't look well."

"I'm sure that won't be necessary. Gwen will take care of everything."

Gwen Archer gave me a sharp look before glancing down at Kayla Barnes. Obviously, she didn't like what she saw. She looked at me again, quizzically.

"Have me met?"

"Ah don't believe I've had that honor."

Anything was possible and our paths could have crossed. While I didn't believe she'd recognize me in my wig and makeup, my stand out albatross could have been familiar. I definitely would have remembered her.

She wore 4-inch heels but was taller than me even without them. She dressed mannish in dark slacks and jacket with an open collared white shirt. Her dark hair was cut short and brushed back. She exuded a cruel beauty: hollowed cheeks and prominent cheekbones. I couldn't be sure which way she was bent, but if I ever wanted a dominatrix she'd fill the bill.

"Charlotte's recently arrived from Biloxi."

Archer dismissed me and knelt by the girl. She made the same checks I had. She stood back up, smiled and glared at the same time.

"She's fine, just too much to drink. I'll have someone take her home. Tomorrow, she won't remember anything."

I'll just bet she won't. "Well, if you are sure she will be all —"

"She'll be fine."

Gwen gave John a get-this-bimbo-out-of-here look.

"Let's go, Charlotte. Everything's under control." John took my arm.

I let him lead me away. I didn't want to leave Kayla Barnes, but couldn't see where I could do anything right then. I had to trust she'd be all right. I wanted to know what happened to her. She hadn't been drinking, of that, I was sure. Most likely she was drugged. My questions would have to wait, even though I didn't feel good about it.

So far I hadn't seen Linda Miller. There was only the slightest hope I would. Jennifer and Barbara had been here twice since the night they met her and hadn't seen her again. I hadn't seen either of the girls either, nor had I seen any photographers.

The girls' descriptions of the parties hadn't prepared me adequately. I don't think they wanted to tell the total truth around PJs. I'm hardly a prude. What shocked me here was how young everyone was. This was a very adult happening with children as participants. Carnivale by Bosch, peopled by Disney. John's comment about the police not being a problem bothered me too. All I could do was pretend to be charmed and keep looking.

We entered a living room. Like everything else about the house, the room was oversized. There were about a dozen adults relaxing, talking and drinking. It was the largest collection of people over twenty-one I had seen so far. You could feel the music vibrating from the other parts of the house, but here it was a quiet background noise only. This was where the grown-ups came to take a break from being chaperones, or whatever they were. A door across the room opened, and a man entered. I got a brief look into the room before he closed the door. I glimpsed someone else seated at a computer. It might be an office.

The man came over to us. He was in his mid-forties with a bit of gray at the temples of his brown hair. He had a trustworthy face and dark eyes. He was casually dressed in a charcoal gray sport coat, black T-shirt and stonewashed black jeans. He didn't wear any jewelry, not even a watch.

John spoke. "Carl, I'd like you to meet someone. Carl Cheswick, this is Charlotte . . . What's your last name?"

"Grey. Charlotte Grey. I am so pleased to make your acquaintance."

"I'm glad you could join us." His voice was an easy, sincere baritone. His handshake warm and friendly. If he were running for office, his smile alone would win him tons of votes.

"Charlotte is from Biloxi. This is her first time here."

"How did you hear of us?"

"Some college students in my apartment building were talking about the parties. They sounded so interesting, I just had to come see for myself."

"Well, I hope you enjoy yourself. This is one of our teen nights. Young people need places to have a good time. I fill that need as best I can. If you would like a more adult gathering, please join us on Monday nights."

"Why thank you, sir. That is so kind. I shall surely plan to do so. This has been—just delightful."

"If you will excuse me, I'll leave you in John's good hands."

"He's so nice. And I am just so surprised at how thoughtful he is. So civic minded, as it were, about today's youth I mean."

"Yeah. Carl's a real prince."

Prince of Darkness, maybe. I couldn't believe the police would let these parties go on. Surely, they knew about them. Frank and I were going to have to talk. The scene here was making me uncomfortable. I wanted to leave, but if I could, I needed to see the rest of the house. I still wanted to find Linda Miller if she were here or get a line on her. I also wanted to find out what happened to Kayla Barnes. Had something similar happened to Linda?

"John," I put my hand on his upper arm. "May we get another drink and finish our tour?"

"Of course. You've seen most of everything down here. Upstairs are mostly bedrooms, although there is a wonderful view of the river from the central balcony."

"Sounds charming. The balcony, I mean. A lady doesn't let a gentleman show her a bedroom on such short acquaintance."

"Then we'll just have to get better acquainted."

Yeah, right.

We went back through the banquet room for margaritas and then headed for the staircase. On the opposite staircase I caught a flash of light. I looked over and saw a photographer taking pictures of two teenaged girls against the balustrade. It was the two who gave me the eye earlier. The photographer didn't look like the description Jennifer and Barbara gave me.

"Who is that taking pictures?"

John stopped and looked. "I think that's Roger Burke. There are usually one or two photographers around. They're always looking for fresh faces."

At the head of the stairs was a smaller banquet room than the one below it. Hallways led off to the left and right. From the left, two young men built like defensive linemen came down the hall giggling and punching at each other. One of them was adjusting his clothes. As they came near, I saw his fly was unzipped. When they noticed us, they stopped their antics. Their faces turned bright red and they passed us with what could only be described as sheepish looks. Had they been in one of the bedrooms playing with each other? Or with another hapless Kayla? I was liking this whole scene less and less.

John led me through the crowded banquet room where a three-piece country group played a rocking version of *Jambalaya*. We went out onto the balcony.

Lights from across the river reflected as constantly changing sparkles on the river's surface. A single black cloud was silhouetted by silver moonlight. On the river beneath it a dark boat glided on the shimmering water. I let the beauty of the scene distract me from the chaos behind me. I recalled paintings by Albert Pinkham Ryder Karen had shown me that looked just like this. Karen would have liked seeing this scene, would have liked painting it. I could picture her joy and passion as she worked a canvas. The thought of her was a lingering ache. Then I pictured Sarah, smiling at me at the weddings, and the ache lessened. She might like this view too. I felt her hand squeezing mine.

"This is beautiful."

"I thought you'd like it."

John's voice startled me. He was holding my hand. I was lost for a moment. I remembered saying "This is beautiful" to Sarah in my thoughts. Apparently, I had said it aloud. I played it again in my head. I heard my voice. My voice, not Charlotte's. I hoped John hadn't noticed. I placed my other hand over his.

"Why sir, " I coated my words in thick syrup "are you an irredeemable romantic?"

John smiled, leaned in and kissed me. I let it go on. Pressed against him. Pulled him to me like a fly to honey and held him despite his heavy cologne. I had to make him forget my slip. When I felt he was enwebbed, I broke away.

"Sir, you take my breath away. What is a lady to do? I do declare." This lady needed to wash her mouth out.

"Tell me you like me as much as I do you."

"I don't know what to say. You are so exciting." Get me out of here. "But this is a might too quick for this little girl to handle. I must say."

I held my hand just beneath my breasts. I breathed deeply several times, slightly flexing my shoulder muscles so that my breasts heaved forward even more so with every intake of air. I moved my hand to his chest.

"I think I better go now. Before this gets beyond our control. Please understand."

"Can I call you?"

"It would be best if I call you. My phone isn't in yet."

Eight

THE SET-UP AT CARL'S was wilder than I imagined. It was hard to believe it had never been raided. Those Sodom and Gomorrah protesters should have been picketing North River Drive instead of the weddings.

I accomplished nothing. I didn't find Linda or get a lead on her. She could have been there, for all I knew. The place was swarming. She could have been in the crowds or in any of the rooms I didn't go into. I didn't find Calvin either. Maybe the other photographer, Roger Burke, knew him.

And what happened to Kayla Barnes? Had she been *roached*? Was she sexually assaulted? Whatever happened, I doubted it was her idea or done with her consent. Should I have blown my cover and tried to help her? At least I had her address to check on her later.

It was past midnight. I hoped Sarah was still at the Kathouse. What would she think of the way I was dressed? I hoped I didn't smell of John's cologne.

Even risking a speeding ticket, it still took nearly thirty minutes to get to the Kathouse. As I approached I saw flashing police lights and emergency vehicles. That couldn't be good. What happened while I was wasting time at Carl's? An ambulance came toward me with its lights flashing and siren just starting. I pulled over a block before the Kathouse and walked down.

A lot of people were crowded about the street. A TV crew was there. Police had crime-scene tape around a large area of the sidewalk and most of the club's parking lot. Uniformed officers were keeping spectators back. I heard someone say someone was killed and I felt a chill. Two police officers were taking names and addresses and asking questions. In the street, one of the Greek gods I had seen get married earlier was sitting at the back of an ambulance. He was dressed now in a light blue pullover sweater and dark slacks. There was blood and dirt on his sweater and a paramedic was treating a cut over his eye. He was arguing with a plainclothes detective I didn't know and pointing in different directions. I couldn't hear what he was saying, but he was upset. It looked like the detective was asking him to repeat himself, because he kept making the same gestures over and over. Streaks of tears glinted in the lamplight.

I tried to get closer to the taped off area. A police officer in a white paper coverall with paper booties was taking photographs, while another officer similarly dressed carefully placed numbered markers on the ground. The markers looked like place cards at a fancy dinner. At the curb, number 73 marked a pool of blood that had oozed off into the gutter. The blood was shiny black in the light from the street lamp.

A policewoman motioned me back from the tape. "You'll have to step back, please. This is a crime scene."

"What happened here? Was it another beating?"

"Please. Just step back."

I wanted to show her my investigator's card, tell her I had a reason for being here; but what could I say. That I could have stopped this from happening if I'd been here instead of wasting my time at the party house? I didn't think she'd be too impressed considering how I was dressed. She probably thought I was a solicitor from the park. I moved away toward the entrance to the Kathouse.

People huddled in tight little clusters. Fear in their faces and in the way they held themselves. I was afraid one of the gods had been killed. Apollo or Adonis. I didn't know which and I felt responsible.

I saw Elspeth, Eloise and Iris. They were crying and clinging to each other.

"Where's Sarah?"

Eloise looked at me. I don't think she recognized me. Her mascara had run leaving her eyes two dark hollow wells from which black ooze streaked down her face. Like the blood at the curb. Her friends held onto her. "Sarah?" she moaned. "Where's Sarah? Oh, Sarah." She convulsed and they had to hold her up. Fear gripped me.

Elspeth looked at me. "Rachel? Is that you?"

I pulled off the Marilyn wig and held it like a dead chicken.

"Sarah," Elspeth stopped and took a breath. "Gary and Richard (Apollo and Adonis apparently) left the club. Sarah went after them. She wanted to congratulate them again on their marriage. She couldn't have been gone a minute. Then Gary came back screaming for Nine-One-One. He was bleeding. They'd been attacked. Then he ran outside. It happened so fast. We found Gary holding Richard over there. Sarah was at the curb. Oh, Rachel! There was so much blood. They just took them away in an ambulance."

I turned and looked down the road where the ambulance had passed me. Sarah had been in that ambulance. Elspeth hadn't said Sarah was dead. I wouldn't believe it. Don't let her die. If someone must die, please, please, don't let it be Sarah.

Immediate shame filled me, yet I couldn't help thinking it, wishing it. I was numb. The four of us clung to each other.

A police officer asked if we had seen anything or knew the victims. He took our names and addresses and asked us to wait to speak with detectives.

"Who's the detective in charge?"

"Detective Montero."

I gave the officer one of my cards. "If Detective Montero has time, I'd like to speak to him. We'll be inside."

More police arrived as we went into the club. I seated Eloise, Elspeth and Iris and ordered drinks. I was functioning on autopilot. The place was crowded, but each table seemed isolated, subdued. Voices were blurred murmurs. There was no music, no entertainment. A few people seemed perturbed and kept looking at their watches. Mayhem and death was an inconvenience to them. I wanted to hit them. Margo Lane sat at the far end of the bar. He saw me, raised his nearly empty glass and waggled it. I went over and sat on the stool beside him. Dropped the wig onto the bar.

Margo wore a curly blonde wig, silk stockings over his long shapely legs, garter belt and a short ruffled costume. A white sequined top hat was on the corner of the bar. Marlene Dietrich in *Blue Angel*. Had he sung "Falling in Love Again" earlier? My heart ached. I wished I had been there to hear it. Maybe Sarah would have stayed with me—not gone outside. Maybe . . .

Margo's face was drawn. His makeup smeared. The creases around his eyes and mouth were pained, not happy. I saw my expression reflected in the mirror behind the bar, my own smeared makeup and mussed hair. We made a sad pair of Augustes.

"Buy you a beer?"

I was glad he didn't use *The Voice* just then. I couldn't have handled it. I might have killed him and climaxed at the same time.

"No thanks. If you have any single malt, I'll take one. No ice."

He went around the end of the bar, picked up a bottle of Balvenie and a tumbler and set them in front of me. I poured a healthy dram while he got another draft for himself.

I made a hood over the glass with my hands, buried my nose between my fingers and breathed in the liquor's essence.

Lost myself in the faint scent of warm honey. Escaped into the ritual, the savoring of Scotland's gold.

The Scotch was not my favored Glenfiddich, but it would do. For the moment, it would do to carry me away from horror. Scotch is strange. Each tastes distinctly different even when distilleries like Balvenie and Glenfiddich use the same spring water, malted barley and bottling plant. One could never be mistaken for the other. Maybe it's the skills of different potmen, or the different pot-stills they use. Whatever, it's a pleasurable mystery.

I missed any trace of smoky peat there may have been. It's said that to release the full aromas when you nose a glass, you should add a measure of pure water. I wouldn't know. For me, 43 percent alcohol by volume is watered enough. As they say, *"Rome was built on seven hills, but Dufftown stands on seven stills."*

God! What banal crap the mind dredges up to avoid reality. I raised my head.

"I called Phil." Margo said. "She's going straight to the hospital."

Hospital. Hope. Please. Please don't let Sarah be dead. Don't let anyone be dead, I corrected. I drank down the Scotch, refilled the glass.

I didn't know what I was feeling. I didn't know the man who'd been hurt; I barely knew Sarah. Surely, I couldn't be in love with her already. How could I? Yet I had wished another's death over hers. The threat of losing her this soon emptied me. This wasn't the way it had started with Karen. Loving Karen began slow and built over months. She had become my life and love for three years when she suddenly left. I met Sarah only twice briefly in the past two days. I liked her. She seemed to like me. Her smile, the squeeze of her hand, thrilled me. I needed to know her more. There was . . . something . . . a potential something that might turn to love. Something that shattered out there on the sidewalk. She couldn't die. She couldn't! I drank my Scotch.

"I'm going to tell Phil we need to close down."

"What?" I looked at Margo. "No! You can't do that."

"Why not? People are getting killed. This has to stop."

"We don't know that. It will be stopped. We don't *know* anyone's died." Please don't let Sarah die.

"I don't want to close, but what else can we do?"

"Don't do it. Please. Margo, this is war. If you close, whoever's doing this wins. We may never catch them. Never find out why they did it. I don't know if it's hate or greed. My gut says greed. Whichever it is, you won't end it by avoiding it. You have to fight back."

"Maybe you fight back. You're a tough bitch. I'm not. Look around. Do these look like soldiers who can fight a war? Who want to fight a war?"

"You'd be surprised who the fighters are."

"Maybe. I don't know. I just don't want someone else getting hurt. I'm tired of it. I think we should close."

"Closing is what they want. Closing is an insult. It insults you who have suffered and those who have . . . have . . ."

I couldn't face the alternative. I drank my drink and poured another. I knew I should stop. I was wasting good Scotch; my taste buds were as numb as the rest of me. Fuck it. I filled the glass again.

The room had cleared considerably. There were few people left. I had no idea what time it was, how long we sat there. The detective I'd seen at the ambulance sat down beside me. I watched his face in the mirror. He looked tired; like a sad bloodhound with long and saggy features. He picked up my wig, inspected it and moved it down the bar.

"I'm Detective Montero. You're Rachel Cord, I presume?"

"Guilty." I poured another drink.

"Frank says you're good people. This is a hell of a mess."

That went without saying. Margo asked him if he would like a drink.

"Can't. I'm on duty. Is there any coffee?" He turned to me. "Maybe you should have some."

I ignored him and finished my drink but didn't reach for the bottle again.

Margo brought him a cup of coffee and packets of sugar and cream. Montero took a sip.

"Needs sweetener." He reached for the bottle of Balvenie.

"Phil called from the hospital," Margo said.

I didn't remember that. When did that happen?

"Richard and Sarah both died."

The news knifed through me. Why hadn't Margo told me?

"I heard. It's a hell of a mess," Montero repeated.

"Are you going to catch these bastards now?" I glared at him. "Are you going to do your fucking job now that it's too fucking late?"

"We do what we can. We'll catch them. They've made mistakes and murder ups the ante. And Sarah Hastings was a British citizen. Diplomatic pressure will increase the brass' interest. There will be more involvement now, not just me and Lockhart. Frank said you're working this for the owners. Have you found out anything?"

I hated his matter-of-fact attitude. "Not yet. I just started. Still playing catch-up."

"Did you know the victims?"

"Not Richard. Sarah . . . I knew Sarah."

Margo broke in. "Richard was Gary's partner. Gary works here. They got married tonight and we were celebrating. They'd been together several years. I don't know what Gary's going to do."

"I heard about the weddings. It's the talk of the town. My sympathies for your loss." Montero looked at me. "Was Hastings gay?"

"Why? Does it matter?"

"Don't get riled. It doesn't matter to me. But if she is, then the headlines are going to read 'Gays bashed at gay bash.' If she isn't . . ."

He let it hang there. Let it percolate in my Scotch-soaked head. I knew where he was going. Public sympathy. We're making progress, but the average citizen would still rather identify with the death of a straight woman than with that of a lesbian. I knew what he wanted to hear. It curdled my soul. We're all a bunch of bastards.

"No, I don't think so. She was a college student here on a work/study program. As far as I know, she was here with friends from work helping them celebrate."

"That's good enough for me. The Press is still outside hoping for a statement. They've buttonholed anyone who would talk to them, but I don't think they have anything on Hastings yet. Her friends were too upset to talk. This could be my only chance to rattle cages before the brass decides it's too important for a lowly detective. Sorry for your loss."

Montero finished his coffee, picked up the bottle of Balvenie and read the label. "Nice sweetener. Have to get me some."

Nine

"Uh, HELLO? WHO IS THIS? Do you know what time it is?"

I waited. Pictured him awakening. Climbing out of the nightmares that must haunt him and which I had been avoiding.

"Shit. It's you, isn't it? What do you want?"

I didn't answer.

"You can't be serious. You can't possibly . . . I can't believe you're doing this. You're sick."

I know. Make me well.

"I don't need this."

I do.

"This is sick. We lost friends tonight. Richard and Sarah died! Isn't that enough for you? But, no, you want some kind of perverted turn-on. You do, don't you? Christ! Why am I talking to you? I ought to hang up."

Then hang up.

Silence. Waiting.

"You don't turn me on, you know. Women don't attract me. Never have. Especially not cows like you."

I know. I'm udderly disgusting. Talk to me, please. Do *The Voice*. Please. Make this pain go away. Help me forget, deny.

"Say something, God damn it. Why don't you say something? You never say anything."

Silence.

"I'm not going to do it for you. You can't make me do it. Why are you doing this? You are such a sick bitch."

Silence.

"You have no idea what you've done."

I didn't seek this. It just happened. Talk to me.

"Shit. I saw how my voice affected you at the club. It shocked me, I'll tell you that. Thought about it all night. Then you called, and I thought I'd play along. Hell, why not? See what happened. Then I heard you . . . those sounds you made on the phone. I couldn't believe it. It was obscene."

I agree. Now do it. Do it!

"This is surreal. I can't believe . . . can't imagine . . . how a voice could turn someone on like that. I don't mean phone sex. I mean just the sound of a voice. My voice. It didn't matter what I said."

No, it didn't. Do it, please.

Silence.

"I tried it on others. Can you believe that? I actually wanted to see if I could do it again. Wanted to know if I could have that effect on someone else. God! Maybe I'm as sick as you are. Toni, my boyfriend, said it sounds ballsy; but he didn't have an orgasm over it. I tried it on others at the Kathouse. Women, even. They had no idea why I was doing it. None of them reacted as you did."

So do it to me. Do it for you. Indulge yourself. Feel the awesome, complete, total control you have. Make us forget.

"This is sick. Our friends are dead. Why am I talking to you about this? I'm disgusting."

We both are.

"I can't believe I'm even considering this."

Who could?

We waited.

"None of us is an island . . ."

Yes!

". . . entire to ourselves. Each is but a piece . . ."

Thank you!

". . . of the Continent, a part of the Main."

It was happening. His basement chords struck deep within; vibrating me to an ecstasy of oblivion.

"If a clod be washed away by the sea, then we are the less. Just as if a promontory were. Each person's death diminishes me, for I am involved in Mankind."

His voice pulled me, spun me, thrilled me, filled me. The words reached through my pain fulfilling me in their own way. An elegy. A blessing.

"Therefore, never send to know for whom the bell tolls, it tolls for thee. It tolls for me. It tolls for we."

Ten

I LAY IN BED a long time after I awoke. I could see bright blue sky. I heard cars passing. A bird trilled. Two people yelled over the noise of a lawnmower. It wasn't fair. Wasn't right.

The sky should be black with chilling rain. There should be no sounds but mourning. Everyone, everything, should be cowering, huddled in loss. There is no future.

A telephone somewhere rang. The bird still chirped its song. A leafblower replaced the mower. I crawled from my cocoon. The sky was still blue.

Hot shower water beat at me. Pounded me. Each drop tried to force its warmth into me. Tried to thaw the frozen, shattered crystal of my heart.

I wrapped myself in the thick terry robe Karen gave me as a birthday gift. I took her picture from the bookshelf and went to sit on the balcony. The chair was still warm although the balcony was now in shadow. I looked at Karen's face.

"Why, for the umpteenth time, did you leave? No messages, no explanations. I come home and you're gone. I needed to go to San Francisco. It was business. You knew that. My client couldn't afford paying for the whole trip. I tried to save her some money. That's why I stayed with Carrie. I explained it. Nothing happened. We're friends, not lovers. We had a fling back in the Army. It was over long before you. You didn't need to be jealous. You finally said you understood before I left. But then you're gone. Why?"

I stared out across the flowing river. Karen apparently left in a hurry; had taken only some of her clothes, some of hers and my jewelry. She took her paint supplies and a few paintings. Left others. Why?

"Why, Karen? I can understand not taking the furniture, but why leave your books, your computer? Your paintings?"

There seemed no rhyme or reason for what she took or what she left behind. Her things were still here, pretty much as she left them. Waiting for her. Like I was waiting.

"I thought we were happy."

We sometimes argued, like any couple, but always made up. We looked at things differently, but we recognized that that was okay. It was just different. Not right or wrong.

"Why won't you talk to me? Why won't you let me find you?"

Karen's picture stared back at me with that impish smile that seemed to say, "I've got a secret."

"What's your secret, Karen?"

No answer. I closed my eyes and held on to Karen's smiling face until it faded and I pictured Sarah's smile. Her face. Her hazel eyes looking at me with promise. Her chestnut hair shining in the lights at City Park. I held that picture tight within me. Kept that moment alive.

THE APARTMENTS ON NORTH 128th Street were tan stucco buildings around a central courtyard with pool and spa. This one had a fountain out front. A sign read, "Now Leasing," and promised tennis courts and gym as well as the pool and spa and two months free rent with a year's lease. The area catered to students at nearby Cramer College.

My first case as an independent agency involved students from Cramer. It happened a few blocks away in College Park. I looked down the road.

The fountain was bubbling and splashing as I closed the latest copy of U. S. News I was holding. I checked my watch. Tapped my foot. Looked around. The sun had been down for hours. There were few people passing through and fewer lingering. No one was alone except me.

I kept up the pretense of waiting for someone. Lamplight cast my shadow onto a nearby wall. My shadow's breasts seemed to stick out a yard from its body. Maybe it wasn't just the angle of light. I wished again for smaller breasts, but that was for sometime in the future. My neck and back felt the strain. I wanted to head for home – take a long bath – but couldn't. I was a private investigator and I was working.

Five women from Cramer College had been raped and murdered in this park over the past year. The police had few clues, hadn't stopped the killings, or made an arrest. Not that they hadn't tried. None of their stakeouts or decoys panned out. And they weren't sharing information. Sometimes it just takes blind luck and being in the wrong place at the wrong time. I tried to explain that to my client.

"I can't guarantee I'll be any more successful than the police have been, Mr. Talbott."

"I understand that. But I have to do something. Our daughter was all we had. It's killing us knowing her killer is still out there. That he's done it again."

I opened and closed my magazine thinking I better move to another area before calling it quits. This was my sixth night playing victim. It was the only plan I had. Talbott would have to decide if he wanted me to continue.

A uniformed officer came along the path. Two other nights the police had hassled me. With my forward elements, they thought I was soliciting. This one looked to be in his mid-twenties. I hadn't seen him before. He was about six-foot and broadly built through the shoulders. The protective vest under his uniform shirt added to the broadness.

"Excuse me. This isn't a safe place for a woman alone after dark."

"Thanks officer. I was just leaving."

"May I see some identification and ask why you're here?"

His tone was friendly but professional. I glanced at his nametag and badge. His name was Friday. The badge number was 714.

I reached into my jeans and pulled out the student ID for Cramer College I made.

"I was meeting friends, but they haven't shown. I just decided to leave."

He handed back my ID. "As I said, it isn't safe here at night. I'll walk you out."

He put his hand lightly on my arm — like a protector or big brother — and guided me down the path. I began tightly rolling the magazine.

Think of a 12-inch section of broom handle. Hard solid wood. Look at the cross section, at the tight circles of growth rings. It can be a formidable weapon. A tightly rolled magazine is just like that piece of broomstick. Paper is mostly wood pulp. Rolled tightly it has great strength. You can swipe it, jab it, or thrust it to cause a lot of damage. If you doubt its effectiveness, buy a ripe watermelon and a magazine. Roll the magazine really tight. Then plunge the end into the watermelon with all your strength. That's the damage it can do. Unrolled, it's just a magazine. You can even roll it while someone's watching and he'll never see it as a weapon.

I gripped the rolled magazine in the center. The officer's vest would prevent a midsection blow. His radio quietly squawked dispatcher instructions. I hoped I wasn't making a mistake. The name and badge number could be coincidence. But he was leading me deeper into the park, not out.

I jammed the magazine hard into his groin. He stopped. His legs buckled. He bent forward. I spun and pulled his head sharply downward mashing his face against my rising knee. I kicked him in the crotch dropping him like a poleaxed steer.

I pulled out the gun hidden under my college sweatshirt. He lay curled in a fetal ball. I kept my weapon trained on him as I removed his service revolver and restrained him with his own handcuffs. His face was bloody. I keyed his radio and said the words every cop fears to hear.

"Officer down. College Park. East entrance."

The memory of that night is always fresh. His real name was Alan Wilson, a cop wannabe. He worked for the janitorial service that cleaned the police station. Reading the police trash and bulletin boards, he knew when to avoid stakeouts. He had looked like a real cop with all the right trappings, right down to the radio. The women must have trusted him. He looked easy to trust. I don't know why he did it—he never said—and I've left it for others to figure out. I was just glad he was on death row and couldn't do it again.

The memory clung to me as I walked to Kayla Barnes' building. I was afraid she had been someone's victim too. At least she was alive. It was possible she wasn't home, that she was in class or out somewhere, but I didn't think so.

Open walkways on each of the four floors faced the courtyard and pool. There were several people lounging about enjoying the sunny day.

I didn't want to be here. I wanted to be home. Home with my pain, my sorrow. But as I sat on my balcony bemoaning my losses staring at the river, I remembered Kayla. Saw her lying on the chaise in the dark—a crumpled throwaway. I had to find her. See her. Know she was well. I couldn't find Linda, and I wasn't there for Sarah, maybe . . .

The door opened. The girl standing there was wearing red tennis shorts and a yellow top. She looked sixteen with her hair in braids. Either college kids are getting younger, or they just look it. She used a finger to keep her place in the book she was holding. It was a text on microbiology.

"I'm looking for Kayla Barnes."

"She's not seeing anyone today."

I handed the girl my card. "I'm a private investigator. I think she may want to talk to me about last night."

"I don't know." She looked at my card and frowned. "She hasn't come out of her room. Just says she wants to be left alone."

"I understand. Tell her I'm here to help her."

I waited until she returned.

"Come on in. Her room's on the left, the door's open. What's goin' on?"

"We'll tell you about it later."

The room was dark. The blinds closed. A desk lamp had been turned on but illuminated only the desk and the chair beside it. Kayla was a huddle of shadow on the bed in front of the window.

"Close the door, please." Her voice was small and flat.

I sat in the chair. I was lit and Kayla remained in shadow.

"I'm Rachel Cord. I'm a private investigator."

"Connie said you wanted to see me about . . . last night."

I strained to hear her. "Yes. Do you remember last night?"

"Not really." She hesitated. "Did . . . did I do something wrong?"

"No, Kayla. You did nothing wrong. Will you tell me what you remember?"

"I went to a party with friends. Out by the river. We were having a good time. We met some boys. We danced. Ate. Shared a drink. I remember looking at the river from the upstairs balcony. The moon had just come up. It was very dreamy. I don't remember where my friends went. I don't remember anything more."

"What do you remember next?

"Waking up here . . . on top of the covers. It was still dark outside. I was still dressed."

"Anything else?"

She shook her head.

"How did you feel, when you woke up?"

"Nauseous. And . . . and I hurt."

"Where did you hurt? Tell me, please. I want to help you."

"All over. My arms, my face. Down there and . . . and in the . . . back." She began crying. I moved to the bed and held her. "Did I do something bad?"

"No. No. You didn't do anything bad." Someone else did.

I held her for a long time and let her cry. She told me how she had found her panties missing when she felt herself where she hurt the most. She said the area was tender and felt sticky and scummy. She had wanted to shower, throw her clothes away, but more, she wanted to curl up and die. She had crawled under the covers and hadn't moved until I arrived.

I told her how I had found her on the chaise and what I suspected had happened. I held her close, rocked her, as she shivered and cried; her face buried in my bosom. I was sorry I hadn't helped her then. I told her over and over how what happened wasn't her fault. As she calmed, I told her how we were going to go to the hospital to have her checked and treated. I promised I wouldn't leave her alone again. I told her there would be a policeman there to speak with her. To help her. She didn't want to go. She wanted to forget the whole thing. I kept talking, convincing her. This was something she'd never forget.

I found a sweatsuit and fresh underwear for her and put them in a bag. I added a nightgown in case they kept her overnight. I thought she was that distraught. At moments like this a woman needs every scrap of comfort and normalcy she can get. Kayla was going to need lots of support. I called Frank Taylor and told him briefly what happened.

Frank and a female detective from Sex Crimes were waiting at the hospital. The female was Det. Sgt. Kerri Trujillo. She wore a tailored pastel suit that set off her dark hair and eyes and brown skin. She was only five-three but looked like she'd be a real spitfire.

Right now, she was all Hispanic mama and Frank was being a big protecting grizzly bear. He and Trujillo kept assuring Kayla she could handle this, that she was a courageous woman; that they would help her through this ordeal. I stayed and held Kayla's hand during the whole process. Detective Trujillo was empathetic and deft in her interview. She took photographs of Kayla's injuries, apologizing each time for any discomfort she was causing. She took Kayla's clothes and all of the evidence that was collected and said she would get Kayla's bedclothes from her home in case there was trace evidence there. She would also seek a search warrant for Cheswick's house.

Kayla was heavily bruised around the vulva and anus. There was bruising around her mouth and nose as well, and on her arms and legs where she had been held. Traces of semen were found in her vagina and anus, down her legs, on her cheek and in her nose. The doctor tested her for HIV and gave her a tetanus shot. She was terribly distraught, so they gave her a mild sedative and admitted her for overnight observation.

In her room, I helped her shower twice—so she could start to feel clean again—then put her to bed. I took a pill from my purse and put it in one of those paper cups they dispense medications in and gave it to her. It wasn't something the doctors prescribed or she had thought to ask for, but it could prevent a possible problem I didn't think she needed to consider.

We called her parents. Mrs. Barnes said she would fly out in the morning if she couldn't get a flight that night. I gave her my cell number to contact me. As Kayla was falling asleep, her roommate, Connie, arrived and said she would stay with her.

Eleven

FRANK AND I SAT at a table outside Charlie's. Frank had a light snack, for him, while I ate my first meal of the day. I needed to buy groceries.

"Only one dog? What's wrong, Frank? Are you sick?"

"Already had lunch and Lorraine expects me home for dinner. She doesn't like it when I'm not hungry when she cooks."

I understood how Lorraine might be peeved about Frank preferring Chicago hot dogs to her cooking. She was a great cook. She could cook for me anytime. We ate our dogs in silence.

"You look worried. I hope you're not upset about Trujillo. This is her specialty. I was there only because you called me. The crime didn't happen here and the victim doesn't live in this district."

"Trujillo was great. That's not my problem. Sorry if I'm out of it. Things keep piling up. I feel like I'm running in place. I don't know what I'm doing anymore, Frank. This is the first thing I've eaten since lunch yesterday. That's not true. I had a funnel cake at . . ." Oh, God! Sarah.

"You okay?"

"Probably not. I don't know."

"Tell me about it. Are you sleeping all right?"

"Forget it. Finish your dog."

I felt drained and my neck and back hurt. My problem was emotional stress, not lack of sleep. Maybe both. Or just the damn weight of my breasts. Hell, I didn't know. These cases were getting too personal. Maybe it was guilt over Sarah's death. I wasn't there when she needed me. I haven't found the attackers. I could have stopped it. Why can't I find Linda? I'm not in control. Damn it! Now Kayla and her mother. Where did that come from? Where the fuck was Linda, anyway? At least I'd helped Kayla. But I couldn't save Sarah. And I had wanted Sarah, wanted to hold her, to — she was special to me — but I wasn't there. And Karen? Why wasn't I there when she left? I don't need that pain again. I'd buried it. Leave it buried. No. I want to remember our love. But why did she leave? And the weird shit with Margo. What's that all . . .

"Come on, Rachel. Talk to Papa Bear."

I had to laugh. "Not this time. Not yet, anyway."

We talked about the cases. What we knew and what we didn't. It helped straighten my head a bit. Frank had nothing new on Linda Miller or the photographer named Calvin; no answers yet from across the river. He said he'd call Trujillo later to see how she was progressing. The deaths outside the Kathouse were causing a stir.

"Ed Montero was on the noon news; so was Deputy Mayor Barrow with the Police Commissioner announcing a task force. Ed's stressing the tragedy and the deputy mayor's blaming the Kathouse. He called it a 'den of iniquity.' Said it should be closed as a 'hazard to moral health.'"

I hadn't seen the news or read a paper. "Sounds like Barrow's running for mayor."

"Who knows, maybe he is. But he's starting awfully early. It's two years before the next election. Anyway, I need to get home. You going to be all right?"

"I'll be fine. Thanks. Give Lorraine and the kids my love."

I stayed and watched the lengthening blue shadows of the buildings come at me; watched the shimmering red ball of a sun descend out of sight down the center of Cutter Avenue.

My back and neck were really hurting. I had been ignoring my exercises and my body was letting me know it. The straps of my bra were digging in. Could I get a massage this late at Ladies Only? If not, I'd settle for a workout and a hot soak in the spa.

Ladies Only is a fitness center halfway between my office and home. My condo building has a small gym and sauna, but I like the facilities at Ladies Only better. They also provide onsite laundry service so I don't worry about smelly clothes or a stale locker. The place is open 24/7, which fits my schedule. But it would be just chance if there was a masseuse available.

Before leaving Charlie's, I looked up Roger Burke in the phonebook. He was only listed in the business white pages as *Roger Burke Photography*. Just the name and number, no address.

I got his voice mail and left a message as Charlotte; I said I could be reached at my friend, Rachel's, number. I didn't want a problem if he had Caller ID and saw my name. It's getting near impossible to pretend you're someone you're not on the phone these days.

My LUCKY NIGHT. GRETCHEN was at the counter checking her next day's appointments when I walked into Ladies Only.

"Go get undress and shower. I be mit you, shortly."

Gretchen's a 45-year-old certified massage therapist originally from Karlsruhe, Germany. Twenty years ago, she'd been an alternate to the German Olympic weightlifting team. She's six-foot tall, dark hair and eyes, and all muscle. She needs no bra for her A-cup breasts; I envied them every time I saw her.

The massage table was Gretchen's design. Not only did it have the standard cutout for your face, but also at breast level there was an adjustable area that could be lowered for comfort. I eased myself onto the table and waited.

"So, Rachel. How long you neglect yourself?" She gave my butt a resounding smack. I grunted. "Is not good you don't take better care of you. You sag when you come in."

"I've been working."

"You don't take care of you, you can't work. Are the titties comfy?"

"Yes, thank you."

She started with a light rubdown and lotions over my entire body prodding and feeling for trouble spots. She eased the strain in my neck and shoulders. There was a spot in my lower back that hurt, and a knot was developing in my left calf. She worked on me for a long time, both sides. I don't know the various techniques she used, but I was soon in dreamland. Aches and pains and stresses melted away.

"Okay. 'Nother shower and soak in spa: fifteen minutes only. Then home to bed."

I OBEYED GRETCHEN and went straight home without stopping for a fresh bottle of Scotch. Not that I needed it; Gretchen worked wonders. I lay cozily wrapped in my robe and curled on my sofa finishing the mushu pork I had ordered, when the news came on.

"Good evening. Death and marriage in the city lead our top stories tonight. I'm Sandra Young."

"And I'm Gary Bentley. The two people murdered outside a popular nightclub in South Ferry may be the victims of gay bashing. Tanya Waverly is live at the scene."

Waverly (*on camera*): "I'm outside Miss Kitty's Kathouse Kabaret on South River Drive. It's quiet now. Flickering candles, flowers and tokens of affection lie here on the sidewalk and in the parking lot. These should be leftovers of a celebration. Instead they're memorials, and this popular nightspot is closed while a black wreath hangs on the door, because Hatred and Death crashed the party.

"It started with gay and lesbian couples being married in controversial ceremonies yesterday evening at City Park. Later, many of the newlyweds, their families and friends came here to celebrate. Just after midnight, one of those happy couples (*picture of Richard and Gary in wedding togas at City Park*), Richard Douglas, a local architect, and Gary Houseman, an entertainer at Miss Kitty's, left the cabaret. When they arrived here at the parking lot (*camera back to Waverly*), four men wielding clubs or bats attacked them. A woman, identified as twenty-two-year-old Sarah Hastings of England, came out of the cabaret at that time and heroically tried to come to Douglas' and Houseman's defense.

(*Scene shifts to file footage of crowd and police; camera zooms in on pool of blood at curb; an ambulance pulls away, lights flashing; Houseman at the back of ambulance with paramedic and Detective Montero.*)

"Douglas and Hastings were critically injured. The attackers got away before help arrived. Hastings died on the way to the hospital. Douglas died an hour later during emergency surgery. The third victim, Gary Houseman, was treated at the scene and released. Mr. Houseman was unavailable for comment. He is in seclusion with friends at an unknown location."

Waverly (*on camera*): "One might think this attack was directly connected to yesterday's gay marriages. However, that might not be completely true according to city police detective Eduardo Montero."

Montero (*file footage at the scene*): "This was an awful crime. This tragedy has taken two lives. However, we don't believe this attack was instigated by the weddings held earlier. The type of attack and the descriptions of the perpetrators match previous attacks we're investigating. These attacks have been occurring for the past two months. All were in this area; all have a connection to Miss Kitty's cabaret; all were directed at the gay community and are being treated as hate crimes. Tonight's tragedies are only the latest and the first deaths."

Voice (*off camera*): "Why haven't the police been able to stop the attacks?"

Montero: "Not enough information or leads. We do what we can, but budget restraints and a lack of manpower have hindered the investigation."

Voice (*off camera*): "Or is it because all the victims are gay?"

Montero: "I can't address that. Besides, Miss Hastings wasn't gay."

Voice (*off camera*): "And now that people have died?"

Montero: "Things will change. Sarah Hastings, who—let me emphasize, again—*was not* part of the gay community, was a visiting foreign national. I believe that her death will have a direct effect on the tenure of this investigation."

Waverly (*on camera*): "Detective Montero's prophecy was quick to come true. This morning the city administration announced a state, county and city task force to investigate these murders."

Vincent Barrow (*file footage from City Hall*): "As deputy mayor, I speak for the whole city. These heinous crimes will not be tolerated. The criminals responsible will be caught. They will be punished to the fullest extent of the law. I've spoken with the governor and he has authorized a task force to lead this investigation. And, acting in the absence of the mayor, I have directed an investigation into the activities at Miss Kitty's Kathouse. This establishment is an insult to families. It is a den of unnatural iniquity and a blight of moral decay. We don't want places like this in our town."

Sandra Young (*split screen with Waverly*): "Tanya, what do we know about the young woman, Sarah Hastings?"

Waverly: "Sarah Hastings was a British citizen. (*portrait of Sarah*) She arrived recently for a work/study program sponsored through Cramer College. She was to start classes in the summer session at the end of the month. She was employed at Philadelphia Long's English Tearoom on Cutter Avenue."

Young: "Do we know why she was at Miss Kitty's last night?"

Waverly: "She was with friends taking part in the evening's celebrations. Although she wasn't gay—as was made clear by the police and later by her friends—she had friends within the gay community that makes up a large portion of the district. Sadly, she had just left the cabaret to congratulate Douglas and Houseman on their marraige when the attack occurred."

Bentley's voice: "Have the police made any progress?"

Waverly: "Some, Gary. The attackers were seen leaving in a blue Chevy van. It is suspected there was a fifth person driving. A blue van was discovered this afternoon (*scene change to van being towed from river*) south of the city by a county deputy sheriff. Apparently, the van was stolen and the attackers tried to abandon it in the river. They were unsuccessful as the water was too shallow due to drought and the van did not completely sink. The police are hopeful they will find evidence in the van leading to arrests.

(*Waverly alone on camera*) "Additionally, the FBI has been asked to join the investigation at the behest of the State Department and the British Embassy. I'm Tanya Waverly for Channel Three TV News."

Young (*at anchor desk with Bentley*): "Thank you, Tanya. There will be a private memorial service tomorrow morning at ten-thirty for Sarah Hastings, the young woman murdered. The private service for family and friends will be held at Philadelphia Long's English Tearoom at 634 Cutter Avenue. Services for Richard Douglas are being planned but have not been announced."

Bentley: "Anyone with information about these killings or the previous attacks are asked to call the police or the 'Crime Stop' number Five-Four-Three-S-T-O-P. Callers may remain anonymous. (*Turning to Young*) This was a truly tragic event."

Young: "Yes it was. Turning now to our other top story. The controversy over the legality of yesterday's gay marriages reached new levels today. Brian Fong has the latest."

I SMELLED FRESH GINGER, five spice and frying tempura batter. I opened my eyes. Karen knelt on the floor dipping shrimp into batter and dropping them into hot oil in an electric wok on the coffee table.

She smiled. "Good. My *makura-makura*, my pillow-pillow girl is awake."

Karen? She's back? I'd given up hope. She wore a white kimono with silver and gold cranes rising into the air. Silver trees bent their bare limbs and gold leaves floated free. Karen's black hair was put up geisha style. Her face was pale. Her brows were perfect, black arches. Her lips were a luscious red. She looked like a picture of her grandmother she'd once shown me.

"Karen. How . . ."

She raised a finger to her lips and shook her head. She poured warm sake into a small cup and gave it to me. I reached for her hand, but she pulled away. She shook her head again.

I sipped the drink. Questions bubbled within me, but each time I tried to ask she shook her head "No."

She fed me tempura shrimp and vegetables dipped in a piquant sauce her mother taught her to make. It was like she had never left. She ate nothing and said nothing. It was surreal. When the meal was finished, she leaned forward and kissed me ever so softly.

I reached for her, but she moved quickly away to the open glass doors to the balcony.

"Karen, where have you been?"

She looked quizzical and then gave me her impish smile. *"Kakushigoto.* That's a secret." She moved onto the balcony and disappeared.

"Karen!" I jumped up.

"These are hot and fresh."

"What?" I turned. Sarah came toward me holding a basket and smiling. The scent of hot baked crumpets filled the room. Her hair was down and still had confetti in it. All she wore was the cameo choker. She pressed a crumpet to my lips.

"Have a tasty bit, love."

My heart pounded and I gasped for air. I sat up. The TV was off. The empty containers of mushu pork and fried wontons lay on the coffee table. The clock said 3:17. I looked through the glass doors onto the balcony and beyond to the river. I felt deserted. Lost.

I checked that the front door was locked, turned off lights, and made my way into bed still wearing my robe. I sat gripping my legs tightly, rocking. I tried not to think. Not to hurt.

Finally, I reached for my cell phone. It rang twice before he picked up.

"I thought you'd call again."

I said nothing.

"I didn't want you to call, yet, strangely, I hoped you would."

I hung up.

I redialed.

Twelve

THE VULTURES AND JACKALS were gathered outside of Phil's. Camera lights, flashes and invasive questions assaulted anyone entering. Vans with satellite dishes clustered along Cutter Avenue. Andy Walther from the *Daily Record* leaned against a lamppost, his back to the crowd. He saw me across the street and raised his pad and gave me a questioning look. I shook my head and he went back to leaning against the post. Gretchen and a female bodybuilder whose name I didn't recall stood at Phil's entrance like immovable lions at the gate.

I wore a man's pinstriped black suit and a slouch hat. Marlene Dietrich in mourning. Or Dietrich doing Marlowe. Or both, I suppose. That is if Dietrich had a double-H bosom. Not that it mattered. It was her attitude I wanted—cocky and aloof—to get me through this day. I bought a copy of *U. S. News* at the corner stand—tightly rolled it—and held it low as I crossed the street and entered the swarm of carrion-eaters.

"Are you—Hey? Watch it!"

"Miss—Oof."

"Were you—Ow!"

"Bitch!"

Gretchen and I shared a smile as I entered the Tearoom.

The memorial service was like so many others: dignified, sweet, yet somehow hollow. Lilies and daffodils surrounded a large portrait of Sarah draped in black. A string quartet softly played Mozart. An older brother managed to be here on behalf of Sarah's family. There was someone from the British consulate. Sarah wasn't there, of course. Sarah wasn't anywhere, anymore. Her body was still at the morgue awaiting pick-up and shipment back to England, but Sarah was already gone.

I let the ceremony wash over me. I made trite sayings of condolences to the brother, to Phil, to Sarah's friends for their sorrow, their loss. But what I felt was my sorrow, my loss, my shame. I couldn't stay through any more. I had to get away. I left through a connecting door to the Tavern and out a side entrance onto Seventh Street to avoid reporters.

I wasn't sure what to do but had to do something or fall apart. I walked north a block, then turned east. Zigging and zagging, block by block, I made my way to River Drive and the Kathouse. I cut through the parking lot. The police tape was gone, but the makeshift memorials were still in place. Fresh offerings had been added, but you could see fading and decay already.

I failed Sarah. I failed Phil. I should have been here. I could have prevented this. I should have known it would happen. That's why I was hired. What I had been paid to do. I hadn't done my job. Now two people were dead. Sarah was dead.

Dead flowers and meaningless tokens marked where Sarah died. The blood was gone, but I could see it—shiny black in the lamplight—the number 73 marking it for eternity in some buried police file. Life was crap.

Why was I here? What did I think I could accomplish? The police scoured the area. Whatever clues there were, they had; whether or not they recognized them as such, as yet. That's the problem. You don't know what's important. What isn't. If it isn't growing or nailed down, you mark it, tag it and bag it. Its importance will come clear later. Maybe.

A neon sign in the window said, "CLOSED." A black wreath hung on the door. I looked across to Riverside Park.

It was another wonderful spring day, which it had no right to be. Families, groups, couples and singles were playing and picnicking and relaxing. A typical Saturday afternoon. They had no idea how close they stood to violent death. Didn't they know this was a day of sorrow, of mourning?

I looked up and down the street. Where had the van waited? The van the killers used; the van hauled from the river. How did the killers know when to attack?

It must have come from the north so the killers could jump out quickly from the sliding side door. How far up the street? I began walking. I'm sure the police did the same thing. I stopped frequently and looked back along the sidewalk toward the Kathouse. The field of view was wrong: straight but narrow and parked cars would have obscured the view. I crossed to the park. This was better. From the parking lot I had a good view of the club's entrance. The lampposts north and south of the club would give good illumination at night.

I walked along the grassy strip back toward the club. When I was nearly parallel with the club I stopped. I hadn't found anything. I turned around. I stepped into the parking lot and began walking north again scanning the ground. No idea what I expected to find, if anything. Again, I stopped frequently and looked back at the club. Somewhere along this lot the killers must have waited.

I was nearly a 150 yards from the club when I found where someone drove across the grassy strip divider onto River Drive. Then I found the stripes of burned rubber on the pavement across two head-in parking spaces. Someone had pealed out in a hurry. I pictured the vehicle parked so the driver had a clear view of the Kathouse. It was a bit far, but maybe the killers had binoculars.

This was where they must have waited. The parking lot hadn't been cleaned recently. Two piles of cigarette butts were on the ground. One where the driver could have dropped the butts out his window; the other where the killers would have tossed them out the open sliding door. There were at least three different brands of cigarettes. I didn't touch anything. The evidence, if I were right, was more than a day old. Maybe the police hadn't searched this far. I pulled out Detective Montero's card and called him.

An hour later, the area was cordoned off and forensic people were putting out their markers, measuring, photographing and collecting evidence. They bagged the cigarette butts, took scrapings and photographs of the tire tracks on the pavement and made castings where the tires ran across the grassy strip. I told my story three times to a captain of detectives, an assistant state attorney and a consulting FBI agent. None of them seemed overly impressed except by the size of my breasts. Their attitudes were "Thank you for your help, now be a good girl and go home so the Big Boys can get to work." Montero volunteered to take me into the station for a formal statement.

"Good thinking about the van." Montero still looked like a sad bloodhound. "We should have searched further. Should have caught it."

"You were pretty busy as I recall. Sorry to disturb you at home."

"No problem. We weren't cooking out 'til later, anyway. I saw you at the memorial service."

"You were there?"

"Lockhart and I were watching the crowd. You'd be surprised how many murderers and arsonists like to see the results of their work. We didn't see any likelies, but you never know. See who looks familiar when we find some suspects."

"So what's your status?"

"Lockhart and I are on the task force. My captain insisted, though I'm no longer authorized to speak to the press. But we took the call on the killings and we did all the work on the previous attacks, so they're stuck with us. Our other cases are on hold until this one's solved. Which is a big change. Gays getting beat up wasn't a high priority. Tourist muggings, prostitutes and flashers — even homeless panhandlers — were more important. As well as robberies, B&Es, domestics and practically anything else. We couldn't get okayed for overtime. There wasn't time or manpower to do it right. I told them this could happen. Now look at the pile of shit we got."

Montero kept up his tirade the entire trip to Police Central. He and Detective Dean Lockhart were temporarily assigned there with the task force. I managed to squeeze in a few questions.

"Why weren't the beatings given priority?"

"Who knows? The emphasis was on the image stuff. City Hall is pushing tourism and 'family values' in a holier-than-thou kind of way. Gays aren't part of the image."

"Were there other gay beatings besides those at the Kathouse?"

"One or two domestics — gay lovers' quarrels. Muggings that could happen to anyone."

"Suspects?"

"Not yet. But when we find them, we'll know it. There are no witnesses except for the victims and little evidence at the scenes. No fingerprints; the attackers wore gloves. Some fibers, a footprint on a shirt where one victim was stomped, hazy descriptions. Like the other night, the perps always dressed alike in blue warm-ups. Like a team. But now they've made big mistakes.

"We found the suits and ski masks in the van they abandoned. The van was stolen from West Side. The owner is a construction worker. He reported it missing yesterday morning. It was gone from his driveway when he came out to go to work. We hope to get hair samples and possibly fingerprints and other evidence from the van. There may be enough saliva on those cigarette butts you found for testing. And Hastings, she scratched one of them. Hand or face, we don't know, but there was bloody skin under her nails."

The thought of Sarah fighting back chilled me. I changed the subject.

"You said 'team.' You mean like football players?"

"Yeah, something like that. That's how the victims described them: built like football players. Even after they started wearing ski masks, later victims gave similar descriptions. Made them look like a team. We've checked all the jocks at Cramer and at State A & M, but drew a blank. We've even asked across the river and at every college within driving distance. We're also checking hate groups, especially the KKK, what with Miss Kitty's initials. Nothing so far. I don't expect anything out of town to pan out, but you gotta look. One thing consistent in all the statements was the phrase 'we don't want fags in our town.' These guys are local, I'm sure. Now we have some support, we'll find them."

Once we arrived downtown, I gave my statement. While it was being typed, I wandered around the conference room the task force was using. On one wall an enlarged map showed where all of the attacks occurred. There were photos of the victims with their names, ages, and the dates and times of the attacks. Strings connected the photos to exact spots on the map. I turned away. I couldn't look at the photos of Sarah and Richard.

There was a whiteboard with descriptions of the perpetrators. Next to it was a tall mannequin dressed in a dark blue warm-up suit and ski mask. On the whiteboard was a dialog bubble like you see in comic strips with its tail aimed at the mannequin. It read "We don't want fags in our town."

Some joker had stuck a Xeroxed photo of Deputy Mayor Barrow on the face of the ski mask. I smiled remembering Barrow's comments from the news. Part of what made it funny was that Barrow was a roly-poly barely over five feet.

Montero gave me the statement to sign. I read it over, initialed each page top and bottom, signed it, and then we left. He offered me a ride but I knew it was out of his way. I said I'd take the bus and sent him off to his family cookout.

I made additions to my notepad waiting for the bus. The pad was amazingly disorganized. Notes on Linda Miller were mixed with those on the Kathouse attacks and my notes on Kayla Barnes. It was a mess—like the inside of my head.

Thirteen

THE BUS DROPPED ME at Cutter and Central Boulevard where I picked up a slaw dog and chili fries at Charlie's and walked to my office. This was my third meal from Charlie's in as many days. I was getting as bad as Frank.

Being Saturday, the building was quiet and dark. I locked the outer door behind me, turned on lights for the stairs and for my end of the hall, and listened to my footsteps echo on the hardwood floors.

There were two folders on my desk and five messages from yesterday. The folders were final reports on two previous cases. One included an additional bill for $600. I went through them quickly, signed the cover letters, and put them in the envelopes Doris or Mary had prepared. I set them aside to put on Doris' desk when I left.

Two of yesterday's messages were from PJs, one was from Rodecker, one from Phil, and the fifth from a Matthew Marston of Marston & Marston, whoever they were. Rodecker's came in at 4:55 p.m. and simply said, "Call me" and left his home number. The two from PJs were "Please call." One was at 11:30, the other at 3:15. Phil's message said she had the "info" I wanted. The Marston one was a cryptic "RE: Business offers."

I called Rodecker.

"Hi, Rachel. Thought you'd like to know we found some photos of Linda Miller like those your friend Taylor told us about. Nothing hard core."

"Where?"

"Street corner stuff. We don't have the photographer yet. We're following some leads. Carson and Jablowski are going to some teen hangouts tomorrow. Carson wants to know if you'd like to go along?"

"Sure. When and where?"

"Nine a.m. at the office. They won't wait, so don't be late."

"Thanks Rod. I'll be there."

I called Phil at home but she wasn't in. I left a message. She wasn't downstairs at the Tearoom either. Elspeth said she had left with Sarah's brother and the man from the Consulate and hadn't returned. There was no one at Marston & Marston. Their message machine gave an emergency contact number or asked me to leave a message. It didn't seem that important. I'd try again on Monday. I called PJs.

"Frank and Stein's Parts. We mix and match."

"Hi, Erica. This is Rachel Cord. Let me speak with PJs, please."

"Yes, ma'am."

"Hello, Rachel. How are you?"

"Stretched too many ways, but hanging in there. I got your messages. Sorry I'm just getting to them now."

"They were from Jen and Barbara. They were going to show you where that party place was, but they hadn't heard from you."

"Right. Sorry, I meant to call. I found out where it was Thursday night and went out there. Then later I got caught up in a death and I forgot all about calling. I'm truly sorry."

"Oh, dear. I hope it wasn't the girl you're looking for."

Maybe it was.

"No. I'm still trying to find Linda Miller. Two people were killed outside a club on River Drive."

"I read about that. That is so terrible. Do they know who did it?"

"Not yet. Ah, PJs. That party house Jennifer and Barbara go to it's . . . it's not a nice place. There's liquor and drugs and no one seems to care. Girls as young as Jennifer were drinking beer and margaritas. One young woman there was drugged and raped without her knowing it. I'd hate to think what could happen to Jennifer or Barbara."

"Thank you, dear. I try to warn them. From listening to them, I suspected as much. But young people don't always listen to advice. They don't believe bad things can happen to them. All I can really do is be here to pick up the pieces and give them some love."

"You do a good job of that."

"Well, I try. And remember, dear, you don't need to be under twenty to get grandmother hugs. You get stretched too thin, you come to PJs."

"Thanks. I will. Talk to you later."

I ate my slaw dog and fries with a diet soda from the fridge. Then I got to work.

I sat at table three, the right hand table of the first row facing the blackboard. Just like being back in Mr. Ramirez's sixth grade class. This was where I had everything pertaining to Linda Miller. In a file folder, there were several 3x5-index cards and a spiral notebook. The index cards highlighted items of interest or questions and were keyed to a page in the notebook. The notebook was a running diary.

I like index cards. When I'm thinking, I can sort them in different ways, spread them out; see different patterns I might not have recognized as such. As I gather information, I don't always know what goes with what. The cards were like playing with a jigsaw puzzle, or playing *Concentration*.

It was sort of like assembling a term paper. Research and notes. Theories and conclusions and areas of further research. Each table was a separate case, a different paper to be written.

There were files on tables one, three and five. Table one was all the stuff I had on Karen and her leaving. I'd go through it now and then to see where I failed; see if I could understand. I don't. I haven't added anything new in months since Helen spoke to her for me, and she told Helen she wanted to be left alone. I should pack the file away, just like I should pack away her things at the condo. But I haven't. Probably won't. On table five was a new file folder, notebook and index cards for the Kathouse attacks and now the murders of Sarah and Richard.

I transferred my scattered notes on Linda Miller into a narrative in the notebook. As I did, I made out occasional index cards: Seen at Cheswick's party Apr. 28; Left with photographer named Calvin (check ID with Roger Burke); She was new in town/went to party with people from bus station/check bus station again. My phone rang.

"Rachel Cord. May I help you?"

"Rachel, dahling. This is Phil. I've just heard your message."

"Hi. Sorry again about Sarah. That was a nice service this morning. I was calling about some information you have for me."

"Oh, yes. You wanted to know who was trying to buy the Kathouse. Have you spoken with Matthew Marston?"

"Not yet. I had a message from him also. Who is he?"

"He's my legal and financial advisor. He came up with three names: Peter McNulty, Tri-X Entertainment, and the Riverside Development Company. Peter owns the Cadillac Club. He's been making offers on the Kathouse for years. He knows I won't sell. It's become a running joke between us. The other two, I'm not familiar with. Matthew says they've made several offers. He has the details, and I asked him to brief you."

"Thanks, Phil. That information will help. I'll get with Marston first thing Monday. One other thing. Will the Kathouse be open Tuesday as usual?"

"I don't know, Rachel. Margo thinks we should stay closed. He told me your thoughts about it. I just don't know. I don't want anyone else getting hurt or killed."

"I don't either, but closing seems wrong."

"Yes, I know, but I'm not certain what is best. The police think it's okay. I need to think about it. Is there anything else you need today?"

"No thanks. I'm really sorry about all of this happening. These . . . people will get caught."

After awhile, I wiped away tears and made cards for the names Phil gave me. Peter McNulty was probably a wash. Tri-X Entertainment sounded suspiciously like Triple-X Video. There was also something familiar about Riverside Development. I'd find out from Marston on Monday.

I went back to work on Linda's file. When I got to my notes on Kayla Barnes, I stopped. Was she a separate issue or part of the Miller case? Both. I wrote a brief comment of finding her at the Cheswick house and added the reference "see Barnes file." Then I put her name in large block letters on an index card and put it on table six behind me. I'd get out a new notebook and start a file later.

The school clock on the back wall said six o'clock. I had called the hospital in the morning about Kayla and spoken with her mother. She said she was checking Kayla out as soon as the doctor saw her. I called Kayla's apartment.

"This is Rachel Cord. Are Kayla and Mrs. Barnes there?"

"This is Connie, Kayla's resting. Isn't this just terrible? God! I am so glad I didn't go to that party. I'll get Mrs. Barnes."

"Hello. Rachel? May I call you 'Rachel'?"

"Yes it is, and Rachel is fine, Mrs. Barnes. I wanted to check on how Kayla was doing."

"Please, call me Reggie. That's short for Regina. Kayla's asleep. She took a pill the doctors gave her. She's still numb, as we all are. She doesn't want to believe this really happened. I don't want to believe it. God. What am I going to tell her father?"

"Is he a strong man, Mrs. Barnes? Reggie. Will he support her?"

"Oh, yes. Roy's wonderful. I know he'll be there for her. But this is going to kill him. She was his baby. His favorite. What those . . . animals did to her . . . oh, God . . ."

Kayla had been drugged with Rohypnol and raped by at least three men while she was unconscious. The physical damage might heal quickly, but what had been done to her would affect her and her family forever. I let Reggie spew out all of the crap—the information—the doctors and the police had filled her with. Let her vent her rage till she wore down.

"Is there anything I can do?"

"Thanks. You've done so much. I don't know what would have happened if you hadn't gone to my little girl. It's okay now. It's going to be okay. I'm taking her home tomorrow. I've made the reservations. It's going to be okay."

I hoped it would be—maybe it would—but it would be a long time coming. We arranged to meet at the airport. I'd have just enough time to do that and then meet Carson and Jabba the Hutt.

I wanted a drink, but I don't keep liquor in the office. I made a few notes on an index card and put it on the table with Kayla's name. Then I finished my notes on Linda Miller.

It took me another hour or so to complete my work. I had moved to table five and finished my notes on the Kathouse attacks. The guilt I felt over Sarah and Richard was still with me. I blamed myself that I hadn't done enough. I knew I might be overly critical, but the realization didn't help any. What did I expect? Thirty hours after being hired, two people were dead. Maybe if I had been more focused I could have done more, or at least been at the scene and stopped the killing. But I was trying to find Linda Miller, too. I wasn't Wonder Woman, but I should have been.

Part of my guilt was wishing Richard's death over Sarah's. Part was not being there and saving them. Another part was the sexual obsession I had for Margo's voice. It was irrational and that shamed me. Just thinking of his voice made my thighs squeeze and made me want to reach for the phone. God, Woman! Get a grip!

I got up and walked around. Grabbed another soda from the fridge. Went back to the table. I sat staring at the blank blackboard.

A niggling thought began teasing at the back of my brain. It was like playing basketball in ninth grade gym class. You're stuck. You can't move. You want to make the shot, but the Amazon guarding you is blocking your chance. You're bobbing and weaving, looking for an opening to shoot or pass. The good players are all covered. You've got to move the ball, but all openings are blocked. Out of the corner of your eye, you glimpse the nerdy girl—the one who can't dribble or walk and chew gum at the same time—waving her arms and shouting "Throw it to me. Throw it to me." Yeah, right. You try to ignore her, but she keeps demanding attention. Aw, the hell with it. Why not?

I stared at the blackboard and let the thought come forward. Slowly, I pictured the whiteboard in the task force conference room. The words "We don't want fags in our town" scrawled on it as a joke. Next to it the mannequin with the deputy mayor's photo pasted on its face. The hulking mannequin padded out to look like a football lineman. Then I saw two college jocks coming toward me down a hallway, giggling and prodding each other. One of them adjusting his clothing, his fly unzipped. The two young men at Cheswick's house.

They fit the descriptions of the attackers. Could they be? Cheswick was connected to Triple-X Video. Was he also connected with Tri-X Entertainment? Cheswick had some kind of influence that kept the police away from his parties. Did that same influence curtail Montero's investigation?

I hadn't gotten a look at the rooms upstairs at Cheswick's. I wanted one now. Charlotte wasn't going to wait for Monday night. She was going now.

I keep a safe in the closet as well as some clothes, a filing cabinet and supplies. In the safe are two guns. One was my grandfather's .45 from World War II. The other is a hammerless Smith & Wesson, model 340PD: a small frame, 12-ounce revolver of scandium alloy that takes full load 158-grain .357 Magnum rounds. I made sure it was loaded and took it and five rounds extra in a speedloader.

Fourteen

DRESSED SLIGHTLY LESS TARTY than Thursday night and with my makeup a bit more subdued, I drove to Cheswick's house. Charlotte was ready to party.

The same guard was at the gate. I gave him my best smile.

"Why, hello again. Do you work every night?"

"Feels like it, sometimes. Sorry I can't let you in tonight."

"Why not? Carl and John said I was welcome anytime."

"Well, there's no party tonight. No one's here. The place is closed up."

"But . . . why? There *must* be a party. It's Saturday night."

He laughed. "I know. That's what everyone else who's shown up keeps saying. But not tonight. It's been cancelled."

"Whatever for?"

"No one told me. Just said no visitors, the party was off, and the house was closed."

"Well, pooh. No party." What now? "So, you're here all alone?"

"Basically. Just me and Dwayne and the dogs."

"Dogs?"

"Two Dobermans Dwayne patrols the grounds with every hour."

Great. Dogs. That's all I needed.

"Well, I guess I should be going then. There must be a party someplace. Night now."

I turned the car around and headed south on River Drive. I pulled over a half-mile down the road to think. Cheswick's place was closed up and everyone gone; the party cancelled. Why? It really didn't matter. I still wanted to see the upstairs. I wasn't dressed for B&E or for avoiding guard dogs. Were the building and grounds wired for alarms? What I was contemplating wasn't exactly bright, it definitely wasn't legal, but it was what I wanted to do. I got out and checked the trunk to see if possibly I had a gym bag there with a change of clothes. No luck.

Momentary discretion won out over frustration. I decided to go home, change and get my lock picks. Besides, there were the dogs. Maybe at 4 a.m. Dwayne and the dogs would be asleep. The place was empty; who would know if he skipped a round or two.

On the way home, I turned on my cell phone to check my voice mail. There was one call from Roger Burke. I pulled over and called him back.

"This is Charlotte Grey. Thank you for returning my call. I just now received your message."

"Yes, Miss Grey. You said you were interested in my photography."

"I am. As I believe I said in my message, I saw you the other evening at the Cheswick estate taking photographs. And I would *so* like to have some pictures made of myself, if that were possible?"

"I'm sure we can arrange something. When would you like to meet?"

"If it isn't inconvenient, I am free this evening."

"As a matter of fact, my plans got cancelled tonight. Would you like to meet at my studio?"

"I surely would."

"Okay. Are you familiar with the city?"

"A bit. And I do have a map."

"Great. My address is 3098 Warrick Avenue in the Gaylord Mall at Warrick and Thirtieth Street. Where are you coming from? Do you need directions?"

"I believe I can find it easily enough. Shall we say about thirty minutes?"

"Fine. I'm the last door at the mall. Just buzz when you get here."

It looked like Charlotte would be onstage a while longer before I did my Lara Croft imitation.

The Gaylord Mall was the same strip mall where the Triple-X Video Arcade was located. It formed an "L" and the businesses on the Warrick Avenue side were more respectable. The Christian Science Reading Room on the corner eased the transition. Looking at it from Warrick, you wouldn't believe it was the same mall. There was a ladies fashion boutique, a shoe store, a florist, a credit union, a pizza take-out place, a sandwich shop, an old-fashioned hardware store and at the end, a door.

The door was weathered oak, faded from the sun. Above the door were large, white enameled numbers, 3098. On the wall was a brass plaque, *Roger Burke Photography, by appointment only*, an intercom and letterdrop. Burke's studio was awfully convenient to Triple-X Video. I imagined the kind of photography this sleazeball did. I pushed the intercom button.

"Yes?"

"It's Charlotte Grey."

"Come on up."

There was a buzzing and clicking sound. I opened the door and entered a narrow hallway with stairs leading to the second floor. Roger Burke was waiting on the landing. I guessed him at twenty-eight or there about. He had thick dark hair pulled back into a ponytail. He had dark bedroom eyes with thick lashes I was sure made young girls swoon and many women jealous. I suspected his tan was more from a salon than out in the sun. It may even have been sprayed on; it looked so perfect. He was five-nine and about 150 lbs. He was wearing a yellow polo shirt and khaki pants. He was barefoot.

"Hi, I'm Roger. Please come in." His smile had a radiance you only see on TV advertising dental whiteners.

"I am so pleased to meet you. Thank you for having me over on such short notice."

The room we entered was his customer waiting area. To my left was a door marked "PRIVATE." In front of me was an oak armoire and roll-top desk. The room opened out to the right. There were three large windows at the end of the room looking out over the parking lot. By the windows was a sitting area composed of a beige and dark blue striped sofa and two chairs, an oak coffee table and end tables. As I faced the windows, an open doorway split the wall to my left to Burke's photo studio. The walls were papered a warm slate, a bluish gray with earthy undertones. On the walls were several of Burke's photographs.

"May I offer you something to drink?"

"Some wine if you have it, please."

"Australian Merlot or German Riesling?"

"The Riesling, if it's chilled. Thank you."

Burke opened the armoire. There was a bar set-up and a small refrigerator. As he opened and poured the wine, I went around the room studying his photographs. There were wedding photos and some landscapes, but most were glamour poses of women, very feminine, very seductive. Provocative without being sleazy. There were no nude photos. Three large photos showed several girls between fifteen and seventeen holding hands and dancing in a park. The impression was of youthful exuberance. It reminded me of a painting.

"Your wine."

"Thank you. Your pictures are lovely, Mr. Burke. Do you do any magazine work?"

"Roger, please. Not as much as I'd like. A few regional magazines, nothing national yet. A few galleries display some of my work and I have a booth at area arts festivals. Most of my work is private commission."

The wine was crisp, slightly sweet with a light straw color. I sat at one end of the sofa. On the coffee table were a wedding album and a glamour portfolio. Burke stayed standing, eyeing me critically. It felt a little strange. I've had men leer, or look in stupefied disbelief. But except for doctors, I've never been examined. It was disconcerting, but that's what Burke was doing. I sat back and tried to appear casual. I sipped my wine. He didn't say anything for several moments.

"Your wig's nice," he said at last. "It frames your face well and helps draw the eye, but I don't think platinum is right for you."

"Why sir, whatevah do you mean?"

"No offense. I think your skin tones and your blue eyes would go better with something redder, darker. What's your natural color?"

In answer, I pulled off my wig.

"Better. But I'd still go darker and redder. And it's awfully short. You need something longer and fuller to better balance your more obvious attributes."

"Are you being insulting?"

"Not at all. 'Artistically critical.' If you want to fix your hair, there's a bathroom to the left through the studio. Then we can discuss what style of photographs you have in mind."

Usually I would have just run my hands through my hair—it's certainly short enough—but I couldn't let an opportunity to check things out pass. I brought along my drink and purse; I didn't want Burke spiking the wine or finding my gun. What kind of girl would he think I was?

The studio was filled with lights, tripods, various backdrops and props, some stools and a red velvet settee. In one corner was a large, two-door, metal locker. The darkroom was next to the bathroom. It was orderly and everything was put away. There were no photos or strips of negatives lying about to whet my curiosity and I didn't have time to search. The bathroom was large enough to have a dressing area and a theatrical makeup mirror in addition to toilet, sink and shower. On a hanging rack were peignoirs, teddies and other lingerie: each in its own cellophane wrapper fresh from the cleaners.

I brushed my hair and gave myself a look over. My self-styled pixie did make my face and head seem small compared to my breasts. Maybe I should let it grow out again. Burke wasn't what I expected. After seeing him at Cheswick's, and thinking about the kiddie porn, I was expecting sleazeball. His hothouse tan and pearly whites wanted to confirm that but didn't jibe with his pictures, which seemed practically works of art.

Four mannequin heads with differently styled wigs were lined up on the coffee table when I returned. They ranged in color from a rich chestnut to an almost black. The styles were all shoulder length and full with varying amounts of wave and straightness. Burke was sitting in one of the chairs and watched me cross the room.

"You're tall," he said. "That helps. Waist and hips are nicely proportioned, but your breasts are—no offense—really overwhelming. One of these should help balance the whole picture. The black may be too dark, but it goes well with the dress you have on. Personally, I favor the auburn."

"I'd like to think I was being insulted, but, after a hard look in the mirror, I'm afraid you may be right. I used to wear my hair long, but I cut it last year in a deep funk. I've gotten used to it. My breasts, well, they've always been a hindrance."

Why was I telling him all this? It was none of his business, and it was difficult trying to stay Charlotte and yet talk about myself.

"I don't believe I have ever had a man be quite so forthright in speaking about my figure."

"I mean no insult, but I do tend to speak my opinions. So, what kind of photos are you looking for?"

"Well. I was thinking I would like some boudoir type pictures. You know, lacy nighties, slightly erotic without being pornographic."

"No nudity?"

"Well, perhaps if it were in good taste, some would be all right."

He nodded. "Renoir or Botticelli, but not *Hustler* or *Playboy*."

"Exactly. You are so perceptive. I am so glad I called you. You know, when I went to that party the other night, I was hoping to meet a photographer. Some friends said I would be a perfect model for one who is often there. His name is Calvin, but I didn't see him. Do you know him, by chance?"

"Calvin Tierney. Sure. He has a studio at his house in Crestwood, across the river. Your friends were right. He does like models with big breasts, but he prefers them young, under eighteen, or at least looking like they're under eighteen. He's also more *Hustler* style."

"Oh dear. Wouldn't that be child pornography?"

"If the models were really under eighteen? Possibly."

"Well, I am glad I didn't meet him then."

"So am I. You're going to be a challenge. Let's take some photos."

"Are you asking me to disrobe, sir?"

"Not at all. And definitely not tonight. For one thing, we haven't made a contract or decided on costumes and poses. For another reason, you're not in the right physical condition tonight for nude photography."

"I beg your pardon?"

"You're wearing a bra and panties and pantyhose, I presume."

"Of course."

"They leave red marks and indentations on the body after they've been worn awhile. Those don't go away quickly and can ruin a pose, even covered by a nightgown. I hate retouching or airbrushing. So, when we shoot—if we shoot—it will be in the morning after a night's rest. You will have freshly showered, you will have dressed in nothing but a robe, and you will bring your clothing and makeup with you. We will do makeup then. Tonight, I just want to take some digital portraits you can take with you to decide which wigs look best."

I left Burke's place much later than expected with a dozen photographs, two each of me in six different wigs. He selected two more wigs as we worked. Afterwards, he showed me his living area where he had more of his work displayed. There were several marvelous black and white photos of nude women and men amid barren landscapes. Those were impressive, as was the fact he didn't hit on me.

Fifteen

CRESTWOOD IS BARELY a dot on the map across the river and eighteen miles north. It has only one building: a combination gas station, convenience store and post office.

Once I knew Calvin Tierney's name and had an idea of where he lived, he was easy to find. Computers are wonderful. I did a search for his number and address. If Calvin was a professional photographer, he didn't advertise in the business or yellow pages. There was only a residential listing. A visit to his County Property Appraiser and Tax Assessor websites gave me details of his property and even aerial photographic views of it and the surrounding area.

Calvin owned a 1992, 1,800-sq. ft. doublewide mobile home on five acres near the end of a cul-de-sac. The house had a 12x24-foot covered deck on the back and an 8x12-foot porch on the front. In addition to the house, there was a 30x40-foot cinder block building that was probably his studio. There was a well and septic system. The house and studio sat in a large clearing in the middle of the property surrounded by woods. The property was 330 feet wide by 660 feet deep. He bought the property in 1999 for $57,000. He had a homestead exemption and his property taxes were $187 annually.

The adjacent properties were individually owned with current taxes paid; therefore, probably occupied. However, the property abutting Calvin's from behind was listed as being bank owned, with no exemptions. Its tax value was $63,925 with taxes owed. It was probably a foreclosure and, therefore, probably empty. It was a 1,600-sq.ft. mobile home built in 2002, with well and septic, also on five acres. Much of the land was cleared for pasture and there was a stable and barn. A mapping website gave me directions and I was pulling into its wooded driveway at 2:43 a.m.

A sign at the road read "FOR SALE, $49,500. See any Realtor for showing." Seemed like a bargain compared to my condo. There was a clear plastic box filled with flyers, but I wasn't interested. I grew up in a rural backwater, but I'm all city girl now. I'd miss the lights, the noises, the people. Especially the people. Weeds and grass grew in the center of the driveway and scraped the bottom of my car.

The house nestled neatly into a grove of live oak. The yard was heavily overgrown. I parked in the carport next to the house facing out for a quick retreat. I left the keys in the ignition and the doors unlocked. I wasn't particularly worried about the car being stolen. The house was clearly abandoned. It was missing skirting around the base and the entry steps were gone. Cinderblocks were stacked to climb up to the front door. I shined my flashlight through a living room window. There were gaping holes punched in the walls and trash all over the floor. I could see into the kitchen and it looked like the dishwasher was missing as well as the stove and refrigerator. Around the side, someone had removed the central heat and air unit, and the well pump and tank were missing. I doubted the bank would get its asking price.

I wore dark jeans, a sweatshirt, a black windbreaker, and comfortable crosstrainers. My ID, cell phone and a lockpick gun were in a fanny pack. My revolver was in one jacket pocket, the speedloader in the other. The moon was above the trees in the clear sky. It was past full but provided plenty of light. I could see the woods of Tierney's property across the pasture.

Frank's smut peddler said the photos of Linda Miller came from this side of the river. Now that I knew where Tierney lived, I believed they were made in his studio. I hoped I would find something there that would lead me to her.

Legally, I had no business here. I should have called Rodecker and passed along the information. I had told him I would. But Rod would have to follow proper procedures, and Tierney's place was in the country, probably out of Rod's jurisdiction. It could take days to check it out properly.

I wasn't waiting days. Sarah died because I took my time. I wasn't wasting any more finding Linda.

I checked to be sure my cell phone was receiving a signal. If I needed to, I wanted to be able to call in the cavalry. I debated calling Tierney to see if he were home. I decided against it. I'd know soon enough if he were there or not.

The grasses and weeds in the pasture were waist high, but there was a sort of trail, so the going was easy. Something large leaped up at me.

I fell backwards to get away. There was scattered movement all around. I scrambled to get my gun out. One good thing about the Smith & Wesson: there was no hammer to get caught on anything. I rolled to my knees and waved my gun in all directions. I caught sight of two flashing white flags bounding off into the woods toward Tierney's. I turned and glimpsed another dark shape with flag raised disappearing across the pasture. My heart pounded and I had peed my pants.

In front of me there was a circular area where the grasses had been tramped down. I had spooked a family of deer bedded down in the pasture. So much for the intrepid detective. I hoped they were as scared as I was.

I crawled through the barbed wire fence at the end of the pasture and entered the woods behind Tierney's house. The undergrowth was thin and I could see the trees outlined by the clearing where the house was. I heard the far-off barking of a dog. I hoped Tierney didn't have any dogs. I forgot to bring treats.

At the edge of the clearing, I stayed in the trees and looked the place over. The block building was off to my left and about a hundred feet closer to me than the house. I didn't see any lights on and I couldn't see any vehicles. There were two small sheds. I moved along the tree line until I could see around the front of the buildings. Still no car and no lights. I went back the other way staying in the shadows of the trees until I was sure I had seen everything.

I entered the clearing keeping a shed between the house and me. Then I moved to the side of the house. I went around it carefully listening at windows. I heard nothing. Whenever I could, I sneaked a peek into darkened rooms. Through a living room window, all I could see was the glow of a digital clock. I saw where Tierney parked his car next to a side entrance. It wasn't there. I was pretty sure he wasn't home.

I went to inspect the studio. There were three windows at one end. The middle one looked like a bathroom window and the others were regular room windows that slid up. They were locked. One window had bars mounted across it. The windows were tightly covered on the inside and there were no lights on and I couldn't hear anything. There were more windows at the back, but these were also covered and locked. I made my way around to the door.

I had delayed as long as I could. It was time to commit a crime. I don't like breaking and entering into other people's places. I've done it. I'll probably do it in the future if I think I need to. Sometimes the results seem justified. Other times they don't. Every time feels wrong.

I slipped the tip of the lockpick gun into the door's deadbolt lock. The gun came with a correspondence course on locksmithing. It works pretty well on cars and most standard locks. I've found it easier to use than individual picks. I pulled the trigger a couple of times and twisted. The deadbolt slid back.

The room was dark. I left the door open and used my flashlight. This was Tierney's studio. There were two stage settings: a bedroom scene and a living room one. There was professional lighting equipment, still and video cameras and video recording equipment. Beyond the set-ups was a door. To my left were three doors corresponding to the windows on that side. The first one had a hasp and padlock. That was the room with the barred window. The middle door opened on a bathroom, as expected. The far door was an empty bedroom. I went back and picked the padlock. Maybe this was where he kept his files.

It was another bedroom. There looked to be someone in the bed. I kept the flashlight covered with my hand letting only a bit of light leak through. I moved to the side of the bed. I saw blonde hair that looked reddish in the glow from between my fingers, and I could see freckles on her nose and cheek. I shined the light fully on her face. It was Linda Miller. She was alive and sleeping peacefully. A rush of relief flowed through me. Then I wondered if she had been used like Kayla.

I tried to wake her, being careful not to frighten her. She didn't want to wake up. Her body was limp. She wasn't restrained. Tierney must keep her drugged. She wore a cotton nightgown. I looked in the closet, but there was no clothing there. I checked the other bedroom and found only a robe. It would have to do. Dressed or not, I had to get her out of there. I didn't know when Tierney might return.

I sat her up and shook her. Tried to get her to wake up and help me. She moaned and murmured "Not now. Go 'way." She only wanted to lie down.

"Come on, Linda. Wake up. You have to wake up. We have to get out of here. Come on. Help me. We have to go."

"Not now. Lemme sleep."

"You can sleep later. Now we have to go. We can't stay here. Put your arm through here. That's a good girl. Now the other arm. Good. Now on your feet. Help me, Linda. I need your help. I'm sorry, Linda, I couldn't find any shoes. We have to go."

She was heavy and weak, and it was awkward getting her up. Our overabundant breasts were a hindrance and tended to push us away from each other.

"Go 'way. Lemme 'lone."

"Come on. It's going to be all right. I'll get you home. We have to go home."

"Home?" She sounded like ET.

"That's right. Home. Come on."

I held her and we staggered through the doorway. I leaned her against the wall while I closed the bedroom door and relocked the padlock. Maybe Tierney wouldn't notice she was missing. I gathered Linda in my arms and turned to help her out of the building when the lights came on.

A man was standing in the doorway. He had one hand on the light switch. The other was pointing a shotgun at Linda and me.

"Stay where you are."

I didn't have much choice. I was burdened with Linda and there was no way I could reach my gun before he shot us.

He was tall, thin and pasty pale: not enough time in the sun. He crossed the room to us. Maybe he would make a mistake so I could do something.

"You're in a lot of trouble, Calvin. Don't make it worse."

His eyes went wide. We had never met, yet I knew who he was. That seemed to worry him.

"Let me take her home, Calvin." I said his name again to keep him off guard. "She won't remember you, and I won't tell. Let me take her home."

He was hesitant. He looked at me and then at Linda.

"Let us leave. No one else has to know. You can do this, Calvin. You can make it right."

He didn't speak. He chewed his lower lip. His nostrils flared as he breathed in air to help him think. I could see the cogs of his mind whirling. It was like watching the wheels of a slot machine and waiting for the final seven to drop. The shotgun barrel began to lower. I freed a hand to get my gun.

"Well, if it isn't Miss Shaa-lot from Bi-looxi. How nice of you to call."

Sixteen

GWEN ARCHER ENTERED the room. Calvin's expression hardened and he pointed the shotgun at us again. Archer gave me her glare/smile.

"You've lost your charming accent. And what have you done to your hair?"

"Let us out of here."

"But you've only just arrived. It wouldn't be hospitable to let you leave so soon." Archer moved closer but didn't get between the shotgun and us. "I thought there was something familiar about you the other night but couldn't place it. The gigantic boobs, of course. And now, without the tarty makeup and wig, the resemblance is even stronger. Are you two—"

"She said she wouldn't tell if we let them go."

"Shut up, Calvin."

"Maybe we should—"

"Shut up, Calvin."

"But she found this place. She knows who I am. What if she tells—"

"LISTEN, worm!" Archer's voice snapped like a whip. She turned and pointed at him. "You DO as you are TOLD!"

Calvin looked away, lowering the shotgun. There was no doubt who was boss. Linda was listless and I had to keep adjusting my hold on her to keep a hand free to reach my gun. Archer turned back to me.

"He's right, Gwen. Let us go. We won't tell anyone what happened. If not, the police will arrest you both."

"Why would the police come here?"

"I told them Calvin had Linda."

"I don't think so. If you told the police, they'd be here, not you."

"The police need a search warrant. I couldn't wait. They're coming."

"I don't believe you. We'd know if they were."

Calvin spoke. "We should let them go."

Archer grabbed his throat and squeezed. Blood oozed where her nails dug into him. "Do—Not—Speak—Again."

I shifted Linda. For a moment she was steady on her feet. I reached into my jacket pocket.

"STOP what you're doing!" Archer pointed at me.

At the snap of her voice, Calvin raised the shotgun and aimed. I could see his eye over the end of the barrel. Two black holes staring at me.

"Show me your hand or he shoots. DO it!"

I pulled my hand out of the pocket and held it out to the side open and empty.

"Put the girl on the floor and take off your jacket. Do it!"

I helped Linda to the floor. She curled up like a puppy and went back to sleep. I took off the jacket and laid it on the floor next to her.

"Take off the fanny pack and put it on the floor. Now turn and lean against the wall. Spread your feet."

I did as I was told. "Gwen, you're making a mistake. The police will—"

The heel of a hand slapped the back of my head and my forehead bounced off the wall.

"Don't speak unless you're told to."

"You won't—"

The hand slapped my head into the wall again.

"I didn't tell you to speak."

She kicked my feet further apart and professionally patted me down. She had done this before. Her hand jammed into my crotch harder than necessary. I was sure she'd done that before, too.

Her lips were close to my ear. "The big cow is wet. Did I scare the piss out of you?"

I didn't answer.

She bounced my head off the wall. "Answer me, bitch."

"Yes." Better to let her think it was she than Bambi and family.

She hit me again. "Yes, what?"

"Yes, you scare the piss out of me."

"Much better. Calvin, come here." I felt the barrel of the shotgun pressed against the base of my skull. "If she moves, kill her. If she speaks, kill her."

I heard Archer moving about the room. My head throbbed making it hard to think. I had no idea how we were going to get out of this. There was the clinking sound of chains. Shackles were attached to my ankles. A hand grabbed my right wrist and pulled my arm behind me. A handcuff closed on my wrist. Then my other hand was shackled and she pulled me away from the wall. She and Calvin held the chains and pulled me over to the bedroom set. They forced me onto the king-sized bed and secured the chains to the bedposts. They stretched my arms and legs tightly.

"Gwen, listen to me."

She slapped me hard across the face. "You listen, cunt. You speak when I tell you to speak." She slapped me again to be sure I understood.

"Fuck you!"

"*Au contraire*, my sweet. *Au contraire*."

She said it quietly and smiled. A finger lightly traced a line down my cheek to my chin. That scared me more than the slaps.

Calvin locked Linda back in the bedroom. Archer sent him to look for my car and to check the area. She picked up my jacket and fanny pack and came over to the bed. She looked at the revolver and speedloader and dropped them on the bed. She studied my ID.

"A private detective. How quaint. What's your relationship to the girl?"

I glared at her. She slapped me.

"When I ask, you answer."

"Her family hired me to find her. What have you done to her?"

She slapped me. "You answer. You don't ask or speak otherwise. I can be nice, or I can be nasty."

She sat quietly on the side of the bed for a few moments contemplating the ceiling. There was a metal framework that held the studio lights. The lights had been turned on and glared. There were lots of pulleys and ropes. The restraints dug into my wrists. The strain to my shoulders was painful. Archer looked at me.

"Why did you come to the party the other night?"

I saw no reason not to tell her. I needed to play for time, to think of some way out of this.

"To find Linda Miller, the girl in the bedroom. Someone told me they saw her there on another night."

"Was that your only reason for being there?"

"Yes."

"Did you know anything about the parties?"

"No. It was the first I heard of them. It just seemed a good place to start looking."

"How did you find this place?"

"I heard Tierney's name and he was seen with Linda. I looked him up on the Internet."

"Okay. Here's nice. We've done nothing with the young heifer except take some pictures. That's all so far. I'm saving her for someone special. Shorty thinks he's a real bull and he likes his women with huge teats ready for milking. He'd probably like you, but he prefers sweet unbred heifers. I like indulging him. He pays really well, but he's been too busy to have her — yet."

I pulled at the restraints. I wanted to strangle the bitch. She was amused by my efforts. There was nothing I could do.

I didn't like that she was being so informative. I didn't think she would have done it, if she thought I'd be able to tell anyone. I really screwed up. I should have had backup. Where was Tonto when I needed him?

"The unconscious girl at the party. Did you have anything to do with her going to the police?"

"Yes. Were you responsible for her rape too?"

"No. That wasn't planned. It just happened. You are such a nosy bitch. I told Carl I thought you were behind the report. You were so concerned about her well-being. Because of you, we cancelled parties, Carl and John have left town for a while, and I, I had to show some cunt cop the entire estate. We barely had enough warning to prepare for her visit. Those were major inconveniences. For that, here's nasty."

Archer hit me full force in the stomach. I couldn't double up because of the restraints. The pain was horrible. If I'd had anything to eat, I would have thrown up. She slapped and punched my face and breasts and drove her fist into my crotch. Her actions pulled at my arms sending daggers into the joints. She pummeled me until I nearly passed out. Blood from my nose ran over my face.

Breathing hard, Archer looked down at me then went across the room and returned with a sharp knife. Reflections from the blade gleamed in her eyes. I sunk away from its touch as she cut my clothes from me. She caressed my breasts with the side of the knife and slid it over my quivering belly to my vulva. She laughed as I uncontrollably peed.

She took two ropes attached to pulleys and tied them around my knees. As she pulled on one rope, she loosened the chain to that leg just enough that my leg was pulled up and outward. She did the same with my other leg leaving me open and exposed; my butt nearly lifted from the bed. I was hurt and scared that she wasn't finished.

She held up a dildo of electric blue silicone. I turned my face away. She smacked it across my belly to get my attention; then forced it into my dry vagina. It burned and pained its way into me. She battered me with it.

Her smiles were evil, but she didn't speak. My torture excited her. She caressed my face, smearing my blood, and kissed me. I wished myself far away. I was humiliated, shamed. I had never experienced anything like this. Something probed my anus. The dildo split me. Tore me. I couldn't hear my screams over the pain. It went on forever. When she pulled it out, its absence felt worse. She shoved it into my mouth gagging me, choking me, suffocating . . .

I COULDN'T THINK where I was. I struggled to remember. My arms ached. I couldn't move them. They were stretched tightly, pulling at the sockets. There was throbbing pain between my legs. I wanted to draw them together but couldn't. My mouth was foul and my jaws hurt. I was afraid to open my eyes.

Something yanked my head back. Held my hair so I couldn't move. A dark shape loomed over me. Warm, salty liquid spurted into my mouth. I gagged. I gulped and swallowed to keep from choking. Archer, naked above me, pissed into my mouth. I twisted my head aside, pulling my hair. Urine splashed my face, stung my eyes. She climbed off of me.

I cringed as Archer caressed my wet face, trailed her hand down to fondle my breast, and then softly massaged my bruised and throbbing vulva.

"There, there, it's all right. My sweet cunt is awake, isn't she? You are my dear sweet cunt, aren't you?"

I hoped she read the hate in my eyes. I refused to speak. She dug her fingernails into me. "Tell me," she said sweetly as she dug her nails in harder.

"I'm your dear sweet cunt." I hissed and hated myself for saying it. The pain ceased.

"You see, Calvin, this cow can be trained."

Calvin knelt on the bare concrete floor. He was also naked. A leather collar was tight around his neck and leather straps were wrapped tightly around his scrotum and erect penis. His penis was a bulging engorged purple-red like one of Charlie's oversized hot dogs. How long had he been like that? How long had I been unconscious? Calvin's face was expressionless. He held himself up straight with his hands resting on his thighs. Nothing stopped him from releasing himself except his own obedience.

Archer tweaked my nipple and I looked back at her. Her breasts were tattooed with blue Celtic swirls. The woad tattoos coiled down her body, around her shaved vulva and down her legs.

"Calvin's been bad. He can't find your car. I've had him waiting for you to wake. Tell me where the car is so Calvin can be released."

"I hope it falls off."

She tapped me lightly on the cheek and I cringed. "Tell me. You don't want *nasty*, do you?"

I began to shake. I couldn't control it. I peed again and couldn't stop. Archer laughed. She enjoyed my fear. Still, I didn't speak. I held out. I knew I would succumb, but I had to know I could defy her first. I had to hold to some scrap of dignity.

"Calvin, bring me the pliers."

"What?" escaped my lips before I could stop it.

A tight chain ran from Calvin's neck collar down his back, between the crack of his ass, and to the straps around his scrotum. Every movement choked him and pulled at his testicles.

Archer showed me the pliers. "Where's the car?"

I didn't know what she planned to do. Tears seeped from my eyes. Someone whimpered; I wasn't sure who. I shook my head, silently pleading for her not to hurt me anymore. She reached down to my vulva and I screamed. She held up the pliers and removed the swatch of pubic hair she had ripped out. She waited calmly.

"Where's the car?"

I screamed. Through tears, I watched her roll another swatch of my pubic hair between her fingers. She reached down and soothed the tortured area with her hand. I tried to pull away from her touch. Tried to sink into the mattress. Sink into oblivion.

"My dear sweet cunt. Don't make me hurt you. Where's the car?"

I refused to answer. I clenched my jaw. She was amused.

I screamed and shook. My vulva burned. My arms were being pulled from their joints in my frenzy.

"I'm tired of your screams. Calvin, cram your cock in her mouth so I can't hear her. Don't bite him, dear. I wouldn't like that."

Calvin forced his bloated hot dog deep into my throat, squashed my nose so I couldn't breathe. My jaws ached at his size. I gagged. Then Archer ripped out more of my pubic hair. I tried to scream. Tried to bite. I choked. As soon as the pain let up a bit, she ripped out more hair. She didn't ask me again about the car. I wanted her to ask me about the car. I wanted to tell her about the car. *Gwen, the car's next door.* I couldn't speak. *At the abandoned property.* Couldn't breathe. *Gwen, I'll go get you the car. Stop. Please. You're killing me.* She didn't stop. They were killing me. There was nothing I could do. Shadows, sparks of dying light, were all I saw. I no longer felt the pain. Let me die. I didn't care anymore. Let them kill me. Let it be over. Sorry, Linda.

Calvin pulled away. I drew in great gobs of air, filled my wracked lungs.

Gwen leaned close. "Where's the car?"

"Bitch!" I spit at her.

Gwen's face turned livid. She lost control. She slapped me. Punched me. Beat at me. Raked me with her nails. Pummeled my belly and vulva. I was fading to unconsciousness.

The chains loosened. She jerked me around, violently flopping me onto my belly my legs hanging uselessly over the side of the bed. She beat on my back. New jabs of pain coursed through my legs and arms, awakening me.

"Calvin!" she screamed. "Fuck the shit out of her!"

Calvin attacked me. I didn't have the strength or will to fight him. I heard him choke as the chain to his collar pulled with every thrust. He was totally obedient. He would keep going until he was exhausted or she gave him relief.

Gwen watched from the other side of the bed so she could see our faces. She watched us with hatred as she licked her lips. She squeezed her breast and her vulva enjoying our torture. Calvin's deep thrusts ripped me. Shame, disgust filled me. Why couldn't I die? I clung to the twisted bedcovers.

Something hard was buried in the blanket. It was my speedloader. It was still where Gwen dropped it, forgotten and hidden. Calvin's breathing was ragged, but he didn't stop. Gwen's eyes became unfocused as the bitch got off on the nightmare she created.

I fumbled through the blanket trying to find my gun. It had to be there. I gripped it, twisted it upward toward Gwen and pulled the trigger. The sound of the .357 round echoed through the cinderblock building. Smoke and flame flared as the blast ripped through the blanket. The bullet hit Gwen below her sternum, knocked her backwards. She stayed on her feet. I freed the gun and shot her where I thought her heart would be if she had one.

Calvin was so deep into his torture he didn't even know what happened. I twisted around as best I could. I shot him through his left eye.

A WONDERFUL SMELL roused me from my stupor. It was the smell of burnt blanket mixed with cordite, blood, rancid sweat, piss and shit. It was wonderful because it told me I was alive.

I had no idea how long I laid there. I was still loosely chained to the bed. I could barely move from the pain. Calvin lay on the floor beside me. Even in death, his penis was stiff and purple. My fanny pack was there also. I pulled it over, got out my cell phone, punched in a number.

"Frank, help me."

Seventeen

"How is she?"

"Difficult to say. Physically, fairly well, all things considered. She was brutally raped and tortured. She has a fractured rib and nose, there's deep muscle trauma, but mostly bruises and scratches. She's healing. She should be fine. Her mental state is another story. She seems catatonic but without the muscle rigidity. Refuses to acknowledge anything around her, although I'm sure she sees and hears. Dr. Howard says it's a form of dissociation. The nurses say she's compliant. Lets them feed her or walk her about. She's like a living, full-grown Barbie doll."

"What are we doing?"

"Watching her, encouraging her friends to stay with her, talk to her. Howard was in but can't do much until she awakens. If she doesn't come out of it soon, we'll transfer her to Psych. Sometimes she screams and shakes for no apparent reason. That is, none we understand yet."

"Well, she's had a nasty experience." (*'You don't want nasty, do you?'*)

"There, see how she shakes? She heard you. Something you said set her off. Certain words seem to cause it. Certain touches do the same. This morning a nurse wiped a tear from her cheek and she went into a frenzy."

"HI, RACHEL. IT'S FRANK. Won't you say 'hello?' Come on. Snap out of it. This isn't like you. You're tougher than this. You've always said, 'Life's a bitch and so are you.' You're going to be okay. You done good, you know. You found Linda Miller. She's going back to her family as soon as they get her through detox. Those bastards kept her tranqued on roofies, but she's going to be all right. She wasn't raped, thanks to you. Come on, Rachel. Listen to Papa Bear. Get up out of there. Let's go down to Charlie's and have us a hot dog. (*Calvin forced his bloated hot dog . . .*) Oh, God. Rachel, don't do that. Nurse!"

"RACHEL, DAHLING. Everyone sends their love. We've had some rain this week finally. The garden is doing beautifully. You must come see it and have tea. We need you, dahling. We are keeping the Kathouse open. You were right. We can't let them beat us. There have been no more attacks. Detective Montero says they have leads on the killers, but no one has been arrested. So, please, come back and find these miscreants. Please."

"*MAKURA AIKOUKA.* Hey, pillow lover. What are you doing in here? This is a place for sick people. We should be out in the sunshine."
"She's right, love. Crumpets and tea in the garden. There's the ticket."

"HEY, SOLDIER? Still in bed? On Your FEET! Inspection in fifteen minutes! Let's move it! Is this any way to act? Captain Abernathy would have you on charges goldbricking like this. Okay, have it your way. When you're ready. No rush. Heck, move over, I'll join you in oblivion. You really left

---

me a big mess, you know. There's a sheriff and DA climbing all over me. They want to charge us with helping you get away. Only the amount of porn and other stuff we found is holding them off—for now. By the way, Carson said to say 'Hi.' The flowers are from all of us, but Carson picked them out. I think he likes you. Didn't have the heart to tell him he isn't your type. We can talk again, later. Rest easy."

"IT'S OKAY, BABY. Let me hold you. Let PJs rock you, baby. It's okay. It'll be all right. That's right, baby. That's right. Let me rock you."

"*OOOOH. YOU ARE such a bitch.*"
Twang.
"You haven't called. So I had to come here. *I taste . . .*"
Twang!
"*. . . a liquor never brewed . . .*"
Twang! Twang!
"*. . . from tankards scooped in pearl . . .*"
Twangtwangtwangtwangtwangtwang!

Eighteen

"**A**RE YOU READY to get out of here?"

"More than ready. I've waited all morning and I'm starved for real food. Take me to lunch, Frank. But not Charlie's! Please. Not Charlie's. Maybe someday. Maybe when I can talk about it. Not yet. Okay?"

"Sure. Whatever you want. Are you okay now?"

"I'm fine. I still look like a raccoon, but the bruises are fading; my ribs ache, but I have pills for that."

"That's not what I meant."

"I know. I'm getting there. I saw the shrink, Dr. Howard, again this morning. I'll see her tomorrow at her office. It's shaky, but I'll be okay. Life's a bitch, but I'll handle it."

"What's that?"

"A scarf from Linda Miller's mother thanking me. She also sent a check for $200. She said she'd send more when she can. She can't really afford it. She said when she got the news, it was the best Mother's Day gift she ever received. God. That was Mother's Day. Frank, I didn't call my mother."

"It's okay, Rachel. It's okay. You can call her later."

"I know, but I always call on Mother's Day. They didn't come see me, did they? Did they even call? Do they even know? Never mind. It's all right; I don't want to know if they know or not. Burned bridges and all that stuff. Hey, look, they won't let me walk out of this place, so wheel me out of here. Let's go to lunch."

FRANK DROPPED ME at my condo after lunch. He wanted me to stay with him and Lorraine. He didn't think I should be alone. He was probably right, but I needed to be in my own space. An hour after he left I was restless. I couldn't sit still. I needed to do something or I would just sit there and think. And I didn't want to do that.

My joints were stiff and achy and my side hurt. I walked slowly over to Ladies Only to get in a workout. The walk helped ease the kinks. It was more than a week since I was there; closer to two, and that was only to get a massage. It had rained earlier, but the sky was clear. The air smelled fresh. I took in big gulps as I walked along. Cleaned my lungs of a wasted week's worth of hospital smells even though it made my ribs hurt. The world didn't look all that different. It had moved on without pause, without interest, in the speck of life called Rachel Cord. A week torn from my life, missing in action.

Gretchen had a client but said she could take me in thirty minutes if I wanted a massage. I changed and started my routine but had to stop and start over. My muscles and joints rebelled. I ended up only doing a series of slow and painful stretches before having Gretchen work on me.

She was careful of my cracked rib. Her skillful hands worked the kinks and stresses from my shoulders, back and arms; but I couldn't relax, couldn't enjoy it like I usually did. I don't remember what she talked about as she worked. I kept myself tensed and locked away, afraid. Afraid one of her touches would remind me of something I didn't want to remember. Send me somewhere I didn't want to go.

CURLED INTO MY ROBE on my balcony, I sipped the last of the Glenfiddich. Part of me felt relaxed; Gretchen had done a good job despite my tenseness; deep inside — was another story.

I stared into the dark. Far-off lights reflected, shimmered and danced on the roiling water. The river washed everything downstream while the lights sparkled in one place. It was all illusion. Somewhere, deep below, hidden within the weeds and muck, buried, lurked other things. Things that wouldn't — couldn't — be washed away. Unseen. Unknown. Waiting. Life had moved on, but like the lights on the water, I was stuck in one place. And I dread the horrid things buried within.

I lost more than a week of my life. Everything that happened was clear until the moment I'm half-carrying Linda. That was sometime in the early hours of the ninth, Mother's Day. Mother's Day — more than a week later and I still hadn't called mine. Maybe tomorrow.

I can remember holding Linda, and then everything shuts down. Or comes at me in horrific flashes, turned up from the muddy bottom of my memories. There are hazy recollections, but my next real memory is Thursday, waking up when the nurse's aide brought my breakfast. I can recall hearing conversations, but they don't seem real. They're like dreams. Then four days of trying to piece together what I had lost. I'm frightened, but with Dr. Howard's help I'm getting a handle on it.

Frank told me he kept me talking on the phone the entire time it took him and the others to reach me. He said I passed out only after they arrived. I don't remember. I don't want to. I can't discuss it. I'm not ready to go there.

The Scotch made me feel warm but I was afraid to sleep. Afraid of what lay lurking, waiting, in the muddy depths. The monsters of the ooze were waiting for me, biding their time.

There was a knock at my door. Through the peephole I saw two young black women waiting in the hall.

"Hi. I'm Rasheena and this is my sister, Shoshana. We're Ruth's daughters. Grandma PJs said we had to stay with you." They came in carrying backpacks, two boxes of pizza and salad.

"We brought dinner," said Shoshana headed for the balcony. "This is a pretty place. Is that the river?"

"What do you mean, PJs said you had to stay here?"

Rasheena looked at me. "Grandma said you can't be alone right now. She said if you won't stay with her, then we have to stay with you."

"I don't need a babysitter."

Shoshana turned back from the balcony. "We cook, we clean, we do whatever you need. But mostly, we hug. Grandma said you need lots of hugs."

"Do you girls know what happened to me?"

Rasheena shook her head. "No details. Grandma just said someone did you a job and you shouldn't be alone."

"Something like that happened to our sister, Najja," said Shoshana. "She was messed up for a long while. We know what it's like. We're here to help."

"Thank you both, really, but I don't need anyone to stay here."

"We can't leave unless Grandma says so. You talk to her and see how far that gets you." Rasheena gave me a knowing smile.

"The pizza's hot. Let's eat," said Shoshana.

"I'M TIRED OF YOUR screams. Calvin . . ."
Gwen ripped . . . tried to scream . . . beyond pain . . .
"Calvin, fuck the . . ."
Smoke and flame flared . . . I put the gun against . . .
"Rachel! Rachel. Wake up. You're having a nightmare."

"It's okay, Rachel. Rasheena and I are here. We'll hold you. It's okay."

"That's right. Calm down now. Go back to sleep. We're right here beside you. You're safe now."

"How are you doing, Rachel?"

"It's pretty rough, Dr. Howard. I'm afraid to sleep because of the nightmares. Even when I'm awake, sounds or words or images cause a flashback and . . . I fall apart. It's rough."

"Are you taking your medications?"

"When it gets really bad. I don't like them. They make me feel out of it, not in control. I don't like that. I need to have control of my life, so I don't take them all the time. I need to get back to work. I've lost more than a week, now. That upsets me. I don't consciously remember the attacks. I was a zombie for four days. Then four more days wasted before the hospital released me. I'm sorry, no offense. I know you saw me several times then. You've really helped. But the meds, they keep me from thinking straight. I need to think straight so I can work. Work helps me feel like myself."

"I understand. We could change the dosage, or try something else if you want. It's all right to use them only when you need them. I suggest you at least take them at bedtime to help you sleep. Are you drinking?

"I had a bit last night. It was all that was left in the bottle. I don't think I would have had much more had there been any. I didn't want to get drunk, but I don't know. It was just a familiar comfort. Something I enjoy."

"Try not to depend on alcohol either, and don't drink and use those medications at the same time. It could be dangerous. Is there anyone helping you, staying with you? Is your family here?"

"Two friends are staying with me. I didn't think I needed help, but I guess I do. They'll be there awhile. As for my family, the nicest thing I can say is that we are 'estranged.' Being a lesbian in a small town wasn't easy, and they found it an embarrassment. I couldn't get away soon enough. Now I only call on Mother's Day—which I haven't done—and on my mother's birthday. As for my father and brothers—forget it.

Except for Wally. He and I are closest in age. I think he suspected all along and understood without saying anything; but he left when I could have used some support figuring things out for myself. He went to West Point. Maybe that's why I joined the Army."

"Have you contacted him?"

"No. He's in Iraq. He has enough to worry about."

"Shall we talk about what happened to you?"

"No."

"You know what happened wasn't your fault, don't you?"

"Yes and no. What they . . . did . . . wasn't my fault. But I can't help thinking if I had been quicker . . . or more aware . . . or something, I could have stopped it from happening. I blame myself for getting into the situation in the first place."

"You saved that girl."

"By luck. I was playing Lone Ranger with no Tonto for backup. That was stupid."

"Do you really think you would have done it otherwise?"

"I don't know. I don't know if I had enough information for the police to get a warrant. It was in another state. I was playing a hunch and I was in a hurry. I didn't know enough. I was looking for information and got lucky she was there. Maybe if I had waited, she would have been gone. I don't know. I guess I would have done it the same way again, knowing what I did then and not what I know now."

"Then don't blame yourself for acting on the information you had. You were successful. Concentrate on that."

"I guess. But I feel like my actions have caused four deaths. Two people died because I failed to be at the Kathouse or find out who was doing those attacks. Then two others died because I let myself get into a situation where I had to kill to get out of. I keep feeling it's my fault."

"Rachel, you're human. You have strengths and weaknesses like everyone else. You aren't responsible for everything that happens in the world. You can't be Superman."

"Or Wonder Woman."

"Exactly. You've told me why you identified with Linda Miller. Particularly, your breasts. Your breast size causes you a lot of pain, emotionally, as well as physically. Have you considered reduction mammaplasty?"

"All the time. That's my dream. But it's expensive and I don't have the insurance to cover it. Hospital bills and these sessions are eating big holes in my 'boob' fund, but I need this too. I know that. Especially now."

"I'm glad you recognize that. If you're not ready to talk about the attack, perhaps we can discuss something else."

"Why not."

"You mentioned a relationship you call a *ménage à quartre?*"

"Yeah. Maybe talking will help me understand it. The foursome is me, Karen Tanaka, Sarah Hastings and Margo Lane."

"Sarah Hastings is the English woman who was killed?"

"Yes. This foursome is all in my head, you understand. I know that. I only knew Sarah slightly. We didn't even get the chance to kiss. But we liked each other, and we made a date to meet the night she was killed. I thought something was . . . blossoming between us. That's partly why I feel guilty. If I had met her earlier in the evening, then . . .

"Anyway, Karen Tanaka was my lover for three years. I thought it was forever. She left me eight months ago. Left town without any word while I was away. We'd had a fight, but I thought we'd cleared it up. I tried to keep track of her, to find her. Traced her to Florida. Wrote, but she didn't answer. I had a police friend—a woman who was my commander in Kuwait—go see her. Karen told her she didn't want anything to do with me. I continued to write, but my letters came back. I've tried to forget her. Bury the memories so the pain wouldn't hurt so much. I really thought we were in love and I still miss her so much. I don't understand what happened. I'm still looking for answers. I have everything she left behind exactly as she left them. I guess I've been hoping she'll come home. I haven't been with anyone since she left, not even one-nighters. Hadn't opened my heart to anyone.

"Then I met Sarah. I was beginning to want to be with someone again. Hold someone. Then thoughts of Karen came back. Now Karen and Sarah are mixing back and forth in my dreams and waking thoughts. I see their faces, their bodies, hear their voices, feel their touch. It's very real and I long for each of them. A lost love and a lost maybe love."

"And Margo Lane?"

"A sexual obsession. He's what woke me to what I'd been missing. Made me realize the denial I'd been living. Margo's the transvestite manager of the Kathouse. We met when I went to interview him about the attacks. He has this voice—God, how do I describe it?—that sends me right up the wall.

"I mean . . . have you ever set the bass on a sound system really low so you feel the vibrations? It's something like that, only more so. I can't really explain it. When he uses that *voice*, it's all over. I mean multiple orgasms. Absolute sexual ecstasy. I don't even have to touch myself. His voice does it all. It doesn't matter what he says. He could read names from the phonebook. He doesn't understand this any better than I do, but it excites him too.

"So I call him late at night. I don't say anything. He knows it's me. He speaks. I listen. I get off. Maybe he does too. I don't know. We both hate it—it's so weird—but we both want it. We have no other sexual interest in each other. He doesn't like women. I don't like men. I've never been with a—
" (*Calvin rammed his . . .*)

"Are you all right?"

"Yes. Sorry. I just had a vision of Calvin Tierney raping me. Is this the first time I've actually said that word? That's the way the flashbacks come . . . all of a sudden. I'm all right now. I was trying to say I've never *willingly* had sex with a man, nor do I desire to do so. This thing with Margo is an aberration. That's my foursome: two lost loves, a captivating voice, and me."

"Perhaps we should stop here. We have another session Friday, but I've been asked to sit in on an interview with you tomorrow. What is that about?"

"My lawyer's request. They're trying to charge me with some level of murder. My lawyer won't let them speak with me without her presence. She would like you there to watch me and to help if I have a flashback."

"They can't honestly believe you acted in any way other than self-defense?"

"Who knows what they believe. Someone's trying to float the idea it was a kinky sex party that got out of hand. My lawyer has been avoiding my being interviewed. Delaying it because of what happened and my emotional state and these guilt feelings I have. She's afraid I'll say something damaging they'll try to use against me. Now I'm out of the hospital, it's harder to put the interviews off."

"I agree with your lawyer. I don't think you're ready for any such interview, and my being there could complicate doctor/patient privilege. I would cancel it if you can."

"I'll tell her your recommendation. See if we can put it off awhile longer."

THE LINDA MILLER FILE was nearly complete. I only needed to finish the final report. I left out everything that happened to me. It wasn't relevant and Linda and her mother didn't need to know. They had enough baggage of their own to carry. Besides, I still couldn't face it, much less write it down. Telling Dr. Howard Calvin raped me was as close as I had come to it. I wasn't getting anywhere. I couldn't finish the report, couldn't find the right words. I sat back and stared out the window. Something made my cheek itch and I brushed at it with a finger.

(*"You don't want nasty, do you?"*)

Gwen, sharp and threatening, hovered over me. She caressed my cheek. I shook with the fear of it. Cold sweat bathed me.

What Archer and Tierney did hadn't stopped with their deaths. It was still happening. I lied to Dr. Howard, to everyone, to myself. It was worse than rough. It wasn't getting better. They still attacked me. Came at me constantly when I least expected. The physical pains were nearly gone, but I still felt the burning, the stretching. The fear. The disgust. The shame.

There was an awful smell. I had messed myself. I opened the windows, got fresh clothes from the closet and went down the hall to clean myself.

Back in my office I sat on the loveseat staring out of the window, tears flowing down my face. I wasn't the tough bitch I thought I was. How were Linda and Kayla handling their ordeals? How did other women handle it? How long do the nightmares linger? The images? The crawly feelings that erupt from nowhere, from an innocent touch or phrase? When does the torture end? How long before you get your life back? How do you live with it? I didn't know and I was afraid to find out.

I held my grandfather's gun: a Colt model 1911, .45-caliber, semi-automatic pistol, gunmetal gray with walnut checkered grips. He carried it through France and Germany during and after World War II. It saved his life and he killed three enemy soldiers with it. He left it to me in his will. It held seven rounds in its clip and one was now chambered. I put the barrel in my mouth.

Nineteen

THE PHONE RANG.

"Rachel, it's Frank. How are you?"

"Okay." I set the gun in my lap. "What do you want?"

"Could you meet with me and Detective Trujillo? There are some questions about the Kayla Barnes case. We could use your help. We won't talk about what happened to you."

"That's good. My lawyer won't let me speak about it." I looked at the gun. "Sure, Frank. I can meet you. Where and when?"

"How about the English Tearoom at three o'clock?"

"Fine. See you then."

I picked up grandfather's gun; stared at it, turning it, twisting it. Then I set the safety, removed the clip and unchambered the round. I put the gun back in the safe, tidied the office, closed the windows, took my bag of soiled clothes and left.

It rained earlier and might again, but it was pleasant on the patio at Phil's. The air smelled fresh and clean. I still couldn't get enough clean air. Elspeth was working and we exchanged hugs. She told me Eloise couldn't get over Sarah's death and had gone home to England to be with her family.

Detective Trujillo was relaxed and comfortable in a pastel blue pantsuit. She sipped her tea. Frank looked uncomfortable. Phil's wasn't his kind of place, but he did say he thought Lorraine would like it and he should bring her here sometime.

"Rachel," Trujillo began, "thanks for meeting me. I know you're having a rough time, but there are overlaps in my investigation with what happened to you. I want to nail these guys."

"Me too. Let's see what happens. What can I tell you?"

"After I interviewed Kayla Barnes, I tried getting a search warrant for Cheswick's place. My lieutenant dragged his feet and I got delayed. I didn't get the warrant until Saturday afternoon. We found no evidence of drugs or alcohol. If you didn't know about the parties, you couldn't imagine them ever occurring. The whole place had been rearranged and cleaned up."

"I know. Archer . . . told me."

"You okay?"

"Yeah. Archer said they barely had time to clean the place up. Somehow, they knew you were coming. Archer paid me back for being a nosy bitch . . . Sorry. Give me a moment. Anyway, when I was there, John, I don't know his last name, said they never worried about being raided. I wondered what kind of clout they had."

"His name is John Thornton. He's Cheswick's business partner. He and Cheswick conveniently left town that Friday night. They're on a business trip in the Bahamas according to their lawyers. They're 'cooperating' through their attorneys; which is a crock of shit. They are 'absolutely shocked' by what's happened. They claim the parties were all innocent fun and entertainment. If there were any irregularities or improper goings on, they knew nothing of it. 'Nothing like *this* has ever happened before.' If there were any drugs or alcohol, or any sexual activity involving underage persons, that was the fault of some of the attendees, not them. As Gwen

Archer is dead, sorry, and can't defend herself, they claim she was in charge of everything. They claim they had no idea what else she may have been doing."

"The bastards. They're lying. They were there. They were in charge. I saw it. Damn! You won't be able to arrest them, will you?"

"I need a lot more evidence than I have now. I've interviewed Kayla's friends, who were with her that night, and I have leads on some of the guys they met, but so far I can't link anything directly to Cheswick or Thornton. And I don't think their business trip will end before they're sure they won't be prosecuted for something."

"How can I help you?"

"Tell me everything you saw the night Kayla was raped. Anything you remember. I need to do another search, a more thorough one this time. Maybe they missed hiding something. As you said, they were rushed to clean the place. I'm sure there's evidence there, and I'll find it if I can get another warrant. A broader one, this time, so I can look for stuff besides just the rape. My lieutenant is obstinate. Won't let me go forward without more information. I think he's afraid of rich people and how it may affect his career. I need to justify another warrant."

We talked over salads and sandwiches and tea. Frank would have preferred Charlie's, but he was being brave and I loved him for it.

As Trujillo and I discussed the two young men I saw coming down the hall, Frank suddenly said, "Oh, my God."

"Sorry," he said. "I didn't mean to interrupt, but I just had a horrible thought."

"What was it?"

"It has to do with Tierney's place. It can wait."

"I'll be okay, Frank. Tell us."

"All right. Archer and Tierney were running a child pornography operation. They photographed and taped everything. They even taped what they did to you."

I felt suddenly sick. The thought of videos existing of my ordeal was repugnant. My gorge rose and I swallowed. I had enough trouble with my own memories; I didn't need to think about actually watching it happen. Or have anyone else seeing it. Frank stopped speaking and looked worried.

"I'm okay. Go on."

"There were a lot of tapes and photos. But what happened to the girls and boys afterward? When Archer and Tierney were finished with them?"

I looked at Trujillo then back at Frank. "I figured they were kept drugged like Linda; then abandoned in another city, maybe."

"Maybe. Do you think that was their plan for you?"

"No. They were going to kill me. I knew too much."

"Right. And probably bury you somewhere on Tierney's five acres. It's nicely remote. What I just thought was that might have been their plan for Miller too. Then I thought of all the kids there must have been before Linda Miller, and I envisioned an entire cemetery."

"Madre de Dios."

"Oh, shit."

"Yeah. I pray it's not true, but I'll call Rodecker and have him pass the idea along."

The horror and anger we felt at that moment made us work harder. That there could be children buried out there pushed my assault and thoughts of suicide aside.

I work a lot of runaway cases. Some, like Linda Miller, I find. Others I don't. The missing may not have ever been in my city or they just passed through or otherwise just disappeared and couldn't be found. Some of my files get closed because there is nothing for me to follow up on and I won't keep taking money on false hope.

Frank and Trujillo went over my statement about Cheswick's parties picking up on different details. When we finished, Trujillo felt she had enough to force her lieutenant into agreeing to another search.

They left and I got a fresh pot of tea and found a hidden spot in the garden. I sipped my tea and smelled the aromas of blooming shrubs and flowers. I wasn't feeling any better about myself, but the anger helped. I no longer needed to go back to the office and eat my gun. At least not yet.

Phil found me. We talked about the weather and the flowers. We talked of Sarah and of Eloise leaving. Phil told me they came from the same village; they had been friends all of their lives but not lovers; Sarah's brother, who came to the memorial, was Eloise's boyfriend. Eloise had suggested Sarah to Phil when Phil made her last trip to England. I hoped Eloise didn't blame herself for bringing her friend here and causing her death. Too many people accept blame and guilt that isn't theirs.

Finally, the conversation turned to the Kathouse.

"We've kept the Kathouse open. Margo has had problems keeping performers and workers, even at premium wages. Many of them are still afraid. We all are, even though the attacks seem to have stopped. However, business is up. People want to be seen at the notorious Kathouse. City inspectors are plaguing us, though, looking for violations. I believe our holier-than-thou deputy mayor is urging them on."

"What exactly is his problem, do you know?"

"I have no idea. Perhaps he is one of those born-again fanatics. I'll be much happier when Mayor Durant returns from her Asian jaunt. I miss her. She's a good mayor."

"I guess I better solve your problem and get him off your back."

"No, Dahling. It's too soon after your troubles. You needn't continue your investigation."

"I need the work, Phil. Work is good. Besides, you've paid me already."

"If you think you're ready, Dahling, of course. Detective Montero said the task force is progressing slowly. No one has come forward with any credible information. They still have no suspects or reasons for what happened. Oh, yes. Matthew Marston still has the information you wanted."

We talked a bit more before Phil had to leave. She offered fresh tea, but I had had enough.

I called Montero and left a message. He and his partner were out and no one knew when they would return. I called Marston's office and made an appointment for the next day. I called the *Daily Record* and asked for Andy Walther. He was out also. I didn't leave a message because I didn't want to leave my name. I'd had enough of reporters hounding me for interviews. As a rape victim the police hadn't released my name, but the word was out anyway. So far no one had published it, but the jackals were circling. "Murder at the Porn Farm" was big news. I could just imagine what would happen if the videos of me were leaked.

I don't like reporters generally. They're parasites. They feed off death and personal trauma. "If it bleeds, it leads" is their mantra. And they don't do it for some altruistic need of the "public's right to know." They do it for money. Sell a few more papers. Get a better broadcast rating. Win an award. Raise their advertising revenues. They push and probe and wheedle with their microphones and cameras and questions into the deepest depths of human suffering. Individually, they may be human. With human thoughts and desires and fears. I've met a few: Andy Walther, for one. But once the pack gathers, all trace of humanity disappears. They're out for blood. As a group, they're a heartless, soulless bunch of vampires.

I suppose I'm not much better. I make my living off of human misery also. But I don't put it out there for the world to see, to glory in it.

Twenty

"**I** WAS FOURTEEN and so was my friend. We told the two guys we met we were eighteen, but I'm sure we didn't look it. They were much older, over twenty-one, anyway. We thought we were cool being hit on by older guys. We shouldn't have gone with them, but we did. Still, what they did to us wasn't our fault. We didn't know that then.

"We partied with them. Drank beer. Necked. When they wanted more we said, No, we had to go home. They didn't like that. Called us 'cock teasers.' Said they'd teach us a lesson. One of them took my friend into a bedroom. I don't know what he did to her, she never told me. The guy I was with touched me and pulled at my clothes. I hit him where it hurts, but not hard enough. It only made him mad. He beat me until I had no fight left or was too scared to fight. He pulled my clothes off. He raped me. Then made me suck him and swallow his come.

"Later he made me call myself filthy names; made me tell him how much I loved what he was doing as he raped me with objects I don't remember. I'm still ashamed I did as he said. That I was so scared I didn't resist more. Didn't fight back. It hurt terribly. The more it hurt, the more it excited him. When he was hard again, he raped me again.

"My friend and I never told anyone what happened, not even each other. We were too ashamed. We went with those men, so we thought it was our fault. They told us it was our fault. Called us bitches, whores, worthless sluts. Told us we deserved what we got. We believed them.

"When we were sixteen, my friend fell in love with a boy at school. The first time he tried to kiss her, she freaked out. Later, she committed suicide. No one understood why except me.

"As I grew older, the experience faded but never really went away. I had few relationships with men. They didn't work out. I met my husband when I was thirty. He was wonderful and patient and we were deeply in love. Intimacy and sex were difficult but we managed. It's still a work in progress. We have two children. It wasn't until the birth of my daughter that I remembered my friend and what happened to us.

"I told my husband about it then for the first time. It was the first time I had told anyone. I lived with the horror of that experience buried within me all those years, and it still haunts my darkest nightmares. But now I force it into the light and face it and talk of it. I'm forty-six now and my daughter will be twelve in October. We named her for my friend. We don't want what happened to me to happen to her, to happen to anyone."

There were six of us seated in a comfortable living room in the home that belonged to Joanne, the woman who was speaking. She told her story calmly with inner strength. I had been warned about triggers. Words or descriptions that could "trigger" a flashback to one's own violation, one's own terror. It happened as Joanne spoke. Each time, as I winced at the pain and memory, and tears flowed down my face, I felt a reassuring touch from one of the women beside me. As we shared our stories, the flashbacks came to many of us, and I, in turn, reached out and held the hand of Clare, a seventy-year-old widow who had been raped and left for dead in a field behind her home three years ago, as the memories became too real for her.

We were a shared sisterhood. Each of us had been violated at some time in our lives. We each understood as someone who had never experienced it couldn't possibly understand. The horror lived within each of us. It never goes away. But by sharing it, facing it, we took control of it. Made it something we could live with, to grow from. Like roses rising from a pile of shit.

I told my story. It was the first time I had spoken of it fully. The first time I really faced it. I described detail I didn't even realize I knew: the sheen of perspiration that made Gwen's body glow; the drop of sweat on her left nipple that threatened to fall each time she leaned over me; Calvin's face as I placed my gun against his eye. And I told how the smell and sound of my own pee could trigger a flashback; how yesterday, in my office, I wanted to kill myself.

I WALKED INTO THE OFFICES of Marston & Marston at five-till-one for my interview. An aide led me to a conference room and served me coffee in a bone china cup with saucer. There was a large oak table with ten leather-backed oak club chairs. One wall was filled with law books from floor to ceiling. On the opposite wall hung a large LCD flat panel TV. Three windows looked down on City Hall and City Park. The last place I had seen Sarah. I turned away.

The table was old. There were nicks and scratches, ancient cup rings and old cigarette and cigar burns. There were worn spots where people over the years had rested their hands. Yet it gleamed with the dull sheen of well-oiled care.

"Good afternoon, Miss Cord. I'm Matthew Marston. I'm sorry if I've kept you waiting."

"I've only been here a few moments. Thank you for seeing me."

Marston was tall and elegant. He was older than sixty. He had thick and wavy white hair and a neatly trimmed mustache. His voice was cool and cultured. He reminded me of the actor Michael Rennie. He laid a leather-bound folder on the table and let his hand caress the tabletop.

"I saw you examining my old friend. This table was my father's. He bought it and these chairs when he opened his law office decades ago in a four-room suite in South Ferry. I don't know how he afforded it. Even then it must have been expensive, and he was just starting out. But he had a dream of having a firm large enough to need a ten-chair conference table. We've expanded beyond its capacity, but I treasure his dream and the memories of things discussed and decided over this old table. I apologize. You didn't come here to hear me reminisce."

"That's all right. I have an old teacher's desk from the thirties. I often think of the stories it holds of the teachers that used it, of the piles of papers and reports that countless students laid on it."

Marston smiled and sat beside me. His expression turned serious.

"Miss Cord, Philadelphia Long is a valued client. She is also an old and dear friend. Her interests are my interests. We employ a large and very fine detective agency. I advised her our agency had the capacity and experience to fulfill her needs. However, for the moment, she has chosen to use your services and has asked me to give you any information I can."

"Thanks for your honesty. I'm a one-woman shop, that's true, and I have no dreams of growing larger. Philadelphia's faith in me may be overconfident. The police haven't solved the crimes at the Kathouse or arrested anyone, although they have a task force dedicated to the problem. A larger agency can come up with more ideas and cover more bases than I can. I've told Phil that and I've made no guarantees. What I do have is personal interest. Phil's my friend also, and so were some of the people beaten and killed. Whether that's a help or a hindrance, I don't know."

"Philadelphia said you wanted information about those showing persistent interest in buying her cabaret."

"That's right. The recent crimes are being attributed to gay bashing. I think it's being done to force the Kathouse out of business, to force Phil to sell the property. I want to know who could profit from it."

Marston opened the folder and passed me the top sheet. "Peter McNulty. McNulty owns the Cadillac Club, Tarzan's, and half-interest in Brownie's Country Bar. He's made Philadelphia offers for the past nine years. Philadelphia always says no. It's a long-standing joke between them. Recently, he invested in a club/restaurant near Cramer College he hopes to open. I don't think he's serious about the cabaret."

He passed me the second sheet.

"Tri-X Entertainment, Incorporated. The corporation owns three adult entertainment facilities within the city and two nightclubs. They own two adult entertainment facilities in adjacent counties and one across the river. It is a privately held corporation with three principals who are also the corporation's officers. They are Carl Cheswick, president; John Thornton, vice president; and Gwen Archer, secretary/treasurer."

"Gwen Archer's dead. You may have read about it."

"I did. Philadelphia told me of your involvement when you were unable to return my call. I hope you have recovered."

"It's a work in progress. Thank you. I'm sorry to interrupt."

"We discovered a fourth shareholder: Millard Fillmore of Tampa, Florida. An interesting name. Millard Fillmore was the thirteenth President, the 'do-nothing' president. It appears this Mr. Fillmore doesn't do anything either. He doesn't really exist. He seems to be merely a conduit for profit sharing to otherwise unnamed shareholders."

"Isn't that illegal?"

"Probably. It may be a gray area, however, if all taxes are declared."

"Any ideas who he or they might be?"

"Not really. Possibly organized crime. Although one doesn't expect them to pay their taxes or hold such a minor interest. It's also possible these are individuals who don't want direct association with this type of business. By the by, the adult entertainment business appears to be ridiculously profitable. Though now I think of it, it is possible this child pornography operation was laundering money through the legal businesses and padding the profits."

"I know a police detective who would like to hear that idea. What about Tri-X offering to buy the Kathouse?"

"They have made five offers in the past year. The first was at market value just over a year ago, in April. The second offer came in November at ten percent above market value. They made their third offer in March within days after the attack on George Dunn. Another offer was made in April, and the final offer for twenty percent above value was made May third."

"Only four days after the attack on Oral Roberts. Seems awfully coincidental."

"I thought so too."

I read the sheet on Tri-X Entertainment. It was a good fit. I wanted it to be Cheswick and Thornton. When they returned, I wanted to be able to take them down or take them out. For Linda and Kayla, Sarah and Richard. I also wanted to know who was the dummy Mr. Fillmore. Marston didn't rush me. He waited until I looked up.

"There is one more buyer you could be interested in, the Riverside Development Company."

"I think Tri-X is the one I want. It fits the time frames, and the Kathouse would be a good addition to launder more money through. Probably why they were willing to pay above market for it. But, I better look at Riverside too."

"I tend to agree with you about Tri-X. A disreputable organization. On the other hand, the Riverside Development Company is a major builder of luxury townhomes and condominiums. They are building that large complex, The Bluffs at Riverside. They have been buying additional property and have made three offers on the cabaret. The first was last September for market value. The second was at the end of February at five percent above value; and the last one was this Monday. Strangely, their last offer was significantly below value. I'm not sure why. Perhaps they think the recent publicity has lowered the value."

"Phil says business is booming because of the publicity. It could be something else. City agencies are pestering the Kathouse, and our deputy mayor wants to close it as a public nuisance. Maybe Riverside knows about that."

"That's a possibility. There have been other one or two-time offers in the past year, but these seemed to fit your criteria the closest."

"This is fine. Thank you. This is what I was hoping to find. I appreciate your efforts."

"If we can be of further assistance in this matter, please call."

Twenty-One

IT WAS A LITTLE after two in City Park. In my mind's eye I could see us all gathered about the fountain— Richard and Gary in their togas, Janet and Janet singing their love, all of us linked together. I could smell the hot grease of the frying funnel cakes, taste their sweetness. I could feel the powdered sugar on Sarah's cheek; see the joy in her eyes. It was a happy memory and I clung to it.

Then I went back to rereading the reports Marston gave me. Marston must have used his "very fine detective agency" for some of the information. I had dismissed Peter McNulty as a suspect and I felt Marston's report confirmed it. Riverside Development was a relatively new company formed explicitly for the current building project and owned by WorldWide Builders, Inc. of Toledo, Ohio. The local president of Riverside was Lester P. Ambrose, also of Toledo, and also a vice president at WorldWide. Phase I of The Bluffs at Riverside was a forty million dollar project. As Marston said, many properties near and around the Kathouse were now owned by Riverside and were, presumably, to be part of a Phase II. Just how important was the Kathouse? I called the Riverside offices.

"I'm sorry, Mr. Ambrose is unavailable. He's usually at the Bluffs at Riverside site. Would you care to make an appointment?"

"No thank you. It wasn't important." I'd track him down at the construction site.

I looked again at the sheet on Tri-X Entertainment. The more I thought about it, the more it felt right that Cheswick & Company wanted the Kathouse as a money laundering operation. Gwen Archer, at least, had the chutzpah to set up the attacks. But would they resort to murder to get the place? The deaths were probably an accident, but the attacks had been getting more aggressive. It had been only a matter of time before someone died. I pictured again the two young men in Cheswick's upstairs hallway and wondered what he or Archer offered them and others to make the attacks. Had they just gotten a bonus in one of the bedrooms? Was Kayla an extra treat? It would be hard to prove and I couldn't get to Cheswick or Thornton with them out of the country. I called Detective Trujillo and gave her the information I had and the connection between Gwen Archer and Tri-X.

"Thanks, Rachel. That's good to know. I think it proves Archer wasn't just a rogue employee as Cheswick and Thornton claim. I'll see if we can get search warrants for their businesses and books and possibly freeze their assets. That should put pressure on them to be more cooperative. I got my warrant to search Cheswick's house again. We're going out later this afternoon. Thanks again."

I tried Detective Montero again. "This is Rachel Cord. I was wondering how your investigation was going."

"It's going, but where I don't know. How are you doing? I came to the hospital with Frank to see you."

"I'm doing better. Sorry, I don't remember you being there."

"Well, you were out of it. I hope it works out for you. On the investigation, no earth shattering results yet. We have three different DNA results off of those cigarettes you found.

One of them matched results from blood we got from one of the sweat suits in that abandoned van and with skin tissue under Sarah Hastings' nails. The sweat suits also gave up DNA matches for Hastings and Richard Douglas and a fourth individual. A baseball bat in the van had blood traces from Douglas and Oral Roberts. So we're making progress. We just need suspects to match the evidence to. So far our leads are going nowhere."

"What about the van's owner?"

"The construction foreman? I'm not sure. Seems to be a dead end. He's in his early forties; too old for one of the perps. He's also too short; five-six. And, he's from out of town. He's only been here a few months. He and his crew are working that big condo job on River Drive. He called Nine-One-One at six forty-five that Friday morning to report the van stolen. Says he left it unlocked in his drive and didn't check it until he was leaving for work. Claims he must have left the keys in it because he couldn't find them. His wife backs him up. Said he was home all night and that they went to bed around ten. His story sounds a little hinky, but we have nothing saying otherwise. Maybe Lockhart and I will have another talk with him."

I told him my thoughts about Tri-X Entertainment trying to buy the Kathouse and may be behind the attacks. He said he would check it out as a possibility. We traded comments about the Mayor's office being a pain in everyone's backsides, and that politicians should let the professionals do their jobs.

I called Andy Walther at the *Daily Record*. "Hi, Andy. It's Rachel."

There was a pause on his end and I imagined him looking around to see if anyone were listening.

"Hi. How are you feeling? Are you calling to give an interview?"

"I'm doing better. My lawyer says I can't talk about what happened just yet. When I can, I'll give you an exclusive. Right now, I'm looking for a favor."

I waited as Andy thought it over. We traded information now and then. Andy was a feature writer for the paper. He did everything from personality stuff to exposés. He had a nice style and his stories came across well. We met when his wife hired me to see if he were fooling around with other women. I tried my Charlotte Grey routine on him to see if he were interested. He wasn't. I thought he might be gay and it was men his wife needed to worry about, not other women. It wasn't uncommon. That idea didn't pan out either. It turned out he gambled. He was involved in an after-hours office poker game and hadn't told his wife. That's where his time and money were going. He wasn't very good at poker. He finally quit playing and he and his wife worked out their problems.

"What's the favor?"

"Information, of course. I'd like anything you can get me on two companies: the Riverside Development Company and Tri-X Entertainment, Inc. Also, can you tell me what's going on with the deputy major?"

"Sounds like three favors. What about Barrow?"

"He's pushing awfully hard to close Miss Kitty's and ranting and raving in the press. It seems too soon to be a political move."

"It's never too soon for politics. He wants to be mayor, so he's building rapport with the righteous right. What's your interest? Are you involved in those attacks and murders at Miss Kitty's?"

"I'm working for the owners. Can you get me some background on Barrow?"

"Sure. What about these companies? Are they involved in some way?"

"Maybe. They've both been trying to buy the Kathouse. I'm trying to establish if there's a connection between their offers and these attacks."

"Okay. I'll see what I can do. I'm in the middle of a story right now. I'll have something for you tomorrow. Seems like a lot in trade for a simple interview."

"When I can talk, it won't be simple. I promise you. I'll tell you things that'll curl your toes and you can't print in the paper."

"We could always write a book."

"Right. *'The Confessions of Madame Gumshoe'* by Rachel Cord as told to Andy Walther."

"See. We already have a title."

After speaking with Andy, I headed over to the County Administration Building. I wanted to check property records before I went to see Lester Ambrose.

It turned out the Riverside Development Company now owned many of the properties near the Kathouse. Several others were owned by B&B Investments, Inc. Riverside started buying around September, the same time they started making offers for the Kathouse.

Properties that now encompassed the Phase I project had been purchased a year to two years ago. Two of the properties had been taken over by the city through eminent domain and sold to Riverside. Many of the properties had been purchased from B&B Investments.

Most of B&B's purchases had occurred only months before selling to Riverside at a considerable profit. It looked like B&B knew about the proposed projects and jumped in and bought properties before the prices rose. B&B bought four of the properties three years ago at giveaway prices. A quick add-up had B&B making at least a $5 million profit on its investments. A neat trick if you can do it.

I called Matthew Marston. "Sorry to disturb you so soon, sir, but I have a question. Did any of those other offers you mentioned for the Kathouse come from B&B Investments?"

"Yes. They made two offers: one in June at ten percent below value and one in August at full value. Is it important?"

"I don't know. I'm at the County Records building and I came across this company. It owns or owned a lot of property sold to Riverside or will be of interest to Riverside. Yet none of its holdings are more than three years old. That's a quick turnaround on investment. Some of the profit margins look staggering."

"I'm not really familiar with the company. Perhaps I should have someone look into it."

"It wouldn't hurt. It's a curiosity. Thanks for your time. I'll stay in touch."

I never know what I'm going to find or where it'll lead me. Most of the time it means nothing and leads to a dead end or onto a long path to nowhere. That's okay. Ninety-nine percent of detection, whether by the cops or private dicks, is scutwork and not the glamour stuff they show on TV. It's a matter of following and eliminating every trail until you find the right one. We're not rocket scientists.

I had two new pieces of information: B&B Investments and eminent domain. B&B was making big bucks on the quick turnaround of property, and I was looking for a profit angle. They made offers for the Kathouse, but backed off when Riverside started bidding. Their last bid was six months before the attacks started. They probably weren't involved, but they may know something that could lead me onto the right path. They were someone to check out further.

And eminent domain, legalese claptrap for stealing for the so-called "public good." The city wanted to close the Kathouse as a public nuisance. If they succeeded, they might force Phil to sell, or threaten to confiscate the property through eminent domain. The city probably thought luxury townhomes were more in the public's interest than a successful nightclub. I knew the deputy mayor was on a religious tirade, but who else might be pushing things along?

I left County Records with a bag full of papers and cabbed it over to The Bluffs at Riverside construction site. I had the cabby let me off in the Riverside Park parking lot.

I went to a nearby picnic table and took out the sheaf of papers from my shoulder bag. I laid out a property map and the property records I had copied. I looked at them and at the buildings and construction site in front of me. Phase I of the Bluffs was a six-block stretch wholly owned by the Riverside Development Company. Nineteen of the properties making up the site had been bought from B&B Investments.

I looked south toward the Kathouse. The two blocks that included the Kathouse on one end and Sam's Deli & Catering on the other were a buffer zone between the Bluffs site and the earlier renovations made in the eighties. I tried to imagine those two blocks torn down and rebuilt with townhomes and condominiums. Visually, there could be an improvement, but the Kathouse was an institution. A landmark I'd hate to see disappear.

The block the Kathouse was in consisted of eight properties. The Kathouse owned two: the building and its parking lot. The warehouse north of the Kathouse with the "SOLD" sign was on two lots and was owned by someone out in Los Angeles. It was possible a recent sale hadn't made it into the records. Who was the buyer, Riverside or B&B? B&B owned the four back properties facing First Street. They started buying them six months before they made an offer on the Kathouse. Did they make an earlier offer outside the timeframe I requested? I'd have to ask. Riverside Development now owned the properties for the moving & storage company, the auto parts store, and the second-hand furniture store in the second block. I imagined those companies' days were numbered and they'd be moving to new locations or closing. Again, B&B owned the four properties facing First Street. Reuben and Esther Feinstein owned Sam's Deli. They lived in an apartment above their shop.

I hadn't eaten since breakfast, so I packed up my papers and walked across to the deli. A mélange of spices filled the air. There were several tables, but no customers at the moment. The woman behind the counter was in her late fifties and friendly. I ordered a double-corned beef on rye with sauerkraut and mustard and a diet soda to go.

"You must do a good business with the construction site next door."

"Oh, sure. Business tripled when they started working. It's like the old days when the factories were open and my father-in-law first opened this shop before the war. That was World War II; before I was born, but Sam told us stories. Those were the best years, up through the sixties. Then the factories started closing. Other businesses moved in and out, but it wasn't the same. Opening the park helped. Most of our business now is catering. Sundays and weekdays we get people from the park, especially in the summertime. We close early on Fridays and we don't open on Saturdays because of the Sabbath. Now it's booming again."

"So you've been here a long time."

"Sixty-seven years in July. Reuben, that's my husband, was born upstairs. He was born on D-Day at the same time his father waded ashore at Normandy. Sam was one of the lucky ones."

Her eyes went moist and her voice thickened. "There were more than thirty men in his boat, Sam used to say. Only eight made it to shore and most of them were wounded. It was a terrible time."

She refocused on me and beamed. "We raised our five children here and put them all through college, too. Yes, we've been here a long time, and we'll be here a long time to come."

"Really? I heard this block was going to be redeveloped after the construction next door was completed."

"That's true. This and the next block are planned to be shops and small businesses and apartments. There's talk of a supermarket on First Street, but I don't think there's enough room for one. Who knows? We made a deal with Riverside Development Company. We keep this location and have an apartment above it just like now. We're already working with their architects on designs. When they're ready to start construction, we'll do catering for a year from another location and then reopen here. Sam's Deli is staying."

As she made up my order, I looked around. One wall was nearly filled with photographs: snapshots and studio poses, group shots and singles, in black and white and in color, faded and yellowed or crisp like yesterday. All people in the military. One section in the middle of the wall was of the Feinstein family with captions. There was Sam in his WWII uniform with his buddies. One picture was a group shot of an entire platoon. Sam was in the third row and looked older than most of them. Some were only kids. Most of them died in the water at Omaha Beach. Another picture was of Sam and three men, all old and in civilian cloths, wearing medals on their coats. Behind them were rows upon rows of white crosses and Stars of David disappearing into the distance. The caption read "Colleville-sur-mer, France, 1994." There were pictures of Reuben in basic training and in Vietnam. There were digital photos of a Saul in flight gear standing in front of a helicopter in Iraq. The rest of the wall was of unknown soldiers, sailors, airmen and Marines, men and women from World War II, Korea, Vietnam and right up to the present day.

"People come in and see our wall," Mrs. Feinstein said, "then they come back or send us a photo of themselves or of a loved one or a friend. We always find a place for them."

"Will you put them back up in the new place?"

"Of course we will. As long as there's a Sam's Deli, that memorial wall will be there, maybe longer."

I went back to the picnic table and ate my lunch—the bread, dark and chewy with no caraway seeds, the corned beef lean—then headed for the trailer that was the construction site office.

A sign at the gate read "HARD HAT AREA." A gray-haired, gray-uniformed guard came out of his shack holding a clipboard and a yellow hard hat with the word "visitor" on it. The shoulder patch on his left arm said he worked for Acme Security.

"I'm looking for Lester Ambrose. Is he here?"

"His car's still here. You can check in the office. I need you to sign in and you have to wear this everywhere but in the office."

"Thanks. Were you here back in March? There was a mugging late at night at the end of the block by the deli."

"You mean the faggot that got beat up? I heard about it. We couldn't help the police much. We don't keep guards on site at night. Just some dogs runnin' loose in the compound and a drive-by every coupla hours. One of our patrols found the guy layin' in the street. They thought it was a woman cause he was wearin' a dress. Boy, was they surprised."

There was a year-old black Lexus sedan and an older maroon Ford station wagon parked in front of the trailer. Off to the side was a white van with the Riverside logo on the front door. The Lexus had to belong to Ambrose.

Inside was a large room where a secretary was busy typing at her desk. The secretary was in her early twenties with straight dark hair past her shoulders. She was dressed casually in a blue work shirt and jeans. I guessed her bra size as a 36B. My dream of dreams. There were two men standing and talking at the far end of the room wearing hard hats and dusty work clothes. The taller one wore a white hard hat. He was about six foot, deeply tanned and in his mid-forties. He was in good shape but his gut was beginning to sag. The other man was shorter and wearing a red hard hat. He was small, about five-six, but the muscles in his back and arms stretched the material of his shirt. His waist nipped in and his pants were tight over a hard butt. They seemed to be arguing.

"I don't care what my brother-in-law promised you, Nick. You fucked up," the bigger one said pushing his finger at the other's face. "You're supposed to be working for me." He stopped when he noticed me. "We'll talk about this later."

170

The secretary said, "May I help you?"

The shorter man turned and left. He was as old as the bigger man, brown-skinned, not just tanned, with handsome features that were now scowling. He moved like a banty rooster, full of himself. He glared as he passed me and I heard him mutter "*Puta!*" Whore. I wasn't sure if he was insulting me or the man he argued with.

"May I help you?" The secretary said again.

"I'm looking for Lester Ambrose."

"I'm Lester Ambrose," the large man said walking toward me. "How can I help you?"

He surprised me. I expected the president of the company to be wearing a $1,600 suit not work clothes.

"I'm Rachel Cord. I'm a private investigator. May I have a few moments of your time?"

"Sure. Why don't we go back to my office? Can I offer you some coffee or a cold drink?"

"No thanks. I'm fine."

"Shirley, if there are any calls, take a message."

The office was pretty plain: a large desk covered in papers, an executive chair with duct tape covering tears on the back and arms, two metal folding chairs, and an old leather couch. The walls were covered with architect's drawings and layouts of the Bluffs project. There was a bathroom off to the left. Ambrose closed the door to the office and the one to the bathroom. He put his hard hat on the desk and indicated we should both sit on the couch.

"About time the insurance company sent someone, but they didn't say they were sending a beautiful woman."

"I'm not with an insurance company."

"Oh? Then how can I help you?"

"You've been trying to buy Miss Kitty's Kathouse Kabaret."

"What interest is it of yours?"

"I've been hired to look into a few things for the owners. This being one of them."

He leaned back and glanced at the door, taking his time.

"Okay. You're correct. We've made offers. We own or have options on all of the properties in the two blocks to the south of us except Miss Kitty's. We're planning to transition that area into businesses, restaurants and upscale apartments. Something to meld nicely with this project. An uplift of the community you might say."

"And Miss Kitty's won't fit into your scheme?"

He glanced away. "I wouldn't say that necessarily. I've been to Miss Kitty's. They put on a pretty sophisticated show. They've been there a long time and have been successful. Success speaks for itself. I'm more concerned with the building than its use."

"Your last offer was a big drop. Why?"

"Ah! Okay, I see where you're coming from."

He looked away then back at me, then leaned forward with all sincerity.

"Our lawyers won't like my saying this, they'd call it bad strategy, but it's like this. We know Miss Kitty's has problems. The beatings and, now, these murders. Building inspectors and fire marshals and code enforcement harassing them. We know all about that. The State Liquor Board may even get involved. If they were closed, the property could lose a lot of value. We came back with a lower offer to jar them into action; get 'em off the dime. We're hoping they come back and say they'll accept our previous offer or make a counter. It's a buying strategy, is all. We'd like to get the property quickly so we can be ready to build when we're done here. You can tell that to your clients. Just don't let my lawyers know I told you."

"One more thing. Do you know anything about who's attacking people at Miss Kitty's or why?"

He looked away again before looking me straight in the eye. I couldn't tell if it was just a nervous habit or if he was trying to think of an answer.

"No, I don't. I've read the newspaper and seen the news, but I have no idea who did it or why. I hope they catch whoever's doing it."

I thanked him for his time and gave him one of my cards. I gave the hard hat back to the guard as I left and walked south.

I thought Ambrose was lying, but about what? And who was feeding him info on the Kathouse's problems? Whatever was going on, Riverside Development was still on my list. However, that was no reason not to tell Phil about Ambrose's offer. I called her at her home and explained the situation.

"Do you think the offer is legitimate, Dahling?"

"I don't know for sure. I felt he was lying about something. But I told you about the deal Sam's Deli made. Maybe you can make a similar arrangement. An old warehouse like the Kathouse must be a bitch to maintain. If you could get a new building and retain ownership, it might be worth looking into."

"I'll discuss it with Margo and Matthew and see what they think. Thank you for the suggestion. How are you doing, dear? I mean personally."

"Better, I think. Talk to you later."

IT WAS THREE in the morning. I lay in bed, wrapped in my robe, sipping Glenfiddich. Rasheena and Shoshana were asleep in the other bedroom. They had done the shopping and made dinner: tossed salad, down-home fried chicken, mashed potatoes and gravy, collards, and black-eyed peas. Comfort food. If they kept that up, I'd need to exercise every day, but I was glad they were here. They were good friends.

I thought of everyone who knew what happened, who supported me without asking for anything or finding fault. I thought of my new sisters—the five women with whom I shared horror. It would be a hard road, but it was survivable. I began to feel a little better, about life, about myself. I picked up the phone.

"Hello?" It was a strange male voice. "Is anyone there?"

Did I misdial?

"Oh, wait! It's you, isn't it? Don't hang up! I'll get Margo."

"Sorry. That was Toni. I wasn't sure you would call again. I saw you at the hospital. I don't know if you remember."

That, I remember. Thank you.

"Still one-sided conversations. Fine. Give me a minute."

I waited.

"Go. Catch a falling star, get with child a mandrake root...."

MY SOUL SANG me awake. My psyche hummed and buzzed and thrilled at the memory of Margo's voice entering me more deeply, more completely, than he could possibly have done physically. *"I Sing the Body Electric"* – that was me. The first time I read those words was as a title of a Ray Bradbury story; then Karen read me the Walt Whitman poem Bradbury had taken for his title. Margo had stirred me with an ancient poet I didn't know; raised passions I had long denied. I pictured Margo's deep voice speaking Whitman's words— *Ebb stung by the flow and flow stung by the ebb, love-flesh swelling and deliciously aching . . .*

I shakily stumbled naked from my bed to the living room bookcase where Karen smiled with impish delight; paid no attention to Rasheena and Shoshana sitting on the couch; grabbed Karen's dog-eared copy of *Leaves of Grass*; carried it breathlessly onto the balcony and screamed, "YAWP!"

Twenty-Two

AT 11:30, I WAS BACK at Riverside Park watching the entrance to the Bluffs project. It had become overcast with a threat of rain. I had two fresh bagels with lox and cream cheese and a large coffee I bought at Sam's Deli. Mrs. Feinstein had been at the counter as her husband, Reuben, sliced meats in the back. I gave her three photos — one of me with "Hot Rod" and "the African Queen," one of my grandfather in his WWII uniform, and one of Wally's West Point graduation — to add to their wall.

I could see the office trailer. Ambrose's Lexus wasn't there, but the Ford Taurus wagon was. I wasn't sure what I was looking for, or what I expected to see. It looked like a typical construction project: a lot of noise and dust, trucks and dozers and workers.

I was waiting to hear back from Marston and Walther. This was as pleasant a place as any to wait. I ate my bagels, reviewed notes, made changes and additions to what I had learned.

A lunchwagon pulled into the parking lot and opened up. Minutes later a whistle blew over at the Bluffs. Workers filed out of the construction site. Some had lunchboxes or bags, and several headed for the lunchwagon; most lined up at Sam's. As they got their food, they went back to the site or came into the park filling up picnic tables or just sitting against a tree on the grass. Two workers headed my way with sacks from Sam's.

"Hey, Babe. Want some company?" said one with a cocky grin. He had blue eyes and was about twenty-five, six-foot, and heavily muscled.

"Not particularly."

The other man was Hispanic with a heavy black mustache, middle thirties, a shade shorter and not as broad in the shoulders; and, he was polite.

"*Perdón, señorita.* We do not wish to offend. May we share your table, *por favor?*"

"Okay. No offense taken." I react well to polite.

"*Gracias.*"

They sat at the other end of the table and I went back to studying my notes. They took off their green hard hats and set them on the bench. The younger guy had brown hair cut short in a buzz. The older one's black hair was tied in a ponytail. They were deeply tanned and the muscles in their arms stood out like thick cords. I wouldn't want to have to fight off either of them, or meet them in a dark alley. They were covered in dust, but their hands and faces had been washed clean. Before opening their lunches, they reached across the table and held hands, bowed their heads, murmured prayers of thanksgiving and crossed themselves.

I tried imagining the younger one in a dark blue warm-up. He could be mistaken for a college jock. For all I knew, he was one. Just because he worked construction, didn't mean he wasn't in college. Maybe the police were looking at the wrong people. All of the witnesses said the attackers looked like college jocks, football players or weightlifters. That didn't mean it was totally true. The witnesses knew each other. They knew what happened to each other. Margo first used the term college jocks. Maybe the others expected to see jocks and, therefore, that's what they saw and what they reported.

176

It happens. Eyewitnesses are often wrong. They don't mean to be. They want to help. They want to get it right. But sometimes they get it wrong. At best, chasing down bad info is just a waste of time. At its worst, some innocent jerk gets nailed for something he didn't do.

There was no reason the men who attacked Margo and killed Sarah had to be college students. They could just as easily be construction workers. There were a lot of well-built men around me now in the park who could have been her attackers. And a construction foreman at this site owned the van that was used. I was looking for a profit motive and Riverside had an interest in buying the Kathouse. Why not use people who already work for you?

"Excuse me. What's the meaning of the different colored hard hats?"

They looked at me, and the older man answered. "The green ones are for skilled labor, like Danny and me. Blue is for common laborers, helpers. Red is for crew chiefs, foremen."

"White hats are for the bosses." Danny added.

"*Si*, that is so."

"Do you know a foreman named 'Nick?'? He's short and he kind of struts when he walks, and he's Hispanic, like you."

"She means 'El Gallo,' Juan." Danny said. He pronounced it like the wine company.

"*El Guy-yo*," Juan corrected. "'The Rooster' we call him. He is the top foreman. He is friend with *El Jefe*, the Boss. But he is not like me. He speaks little Spanish, only vulgarities. He is from Ohio. I am from *Mexico*."

"Do you know him well?"

"No. I have never worked for this company before. But Danny, he worked with him in Ohio."

"He's a real prick. Excuse my language. I only worked his crew once. He plays favorites. If you're not one of his buddies, you get all the shit work. Sorry. I don't like the guy."

"Does he own a blue van?"

"He did, but it got stolen. Mr. Ambrose lets him drive a company van now for him and his pals."

"Are there four of them? Big guys, built like weightlifters?"

"Yeah. How'd you know? Except there are only three now. Jerry Harris went back to Toledo. I heard he had family problems."

"*Perdón, por favor.*" Juan interrupted. "It is time for us to go back to work. Thank you for sharing your table, *señorita*."

"Thank you for the information."

"*De nada.*"

Juan and Danny headed toward the construction site. Many others were headed that way too. Minutes later, a whistle blew and the rest of the workers got up and sauntered toward the gate. I caught a glimpse of a red hard hat.

It was Nick "El Gallo." I thought of it the same way Danny had said it. "El Gallo" was with three big men. They had been sitting at a table about a hundred yards north of me. I couldn't see them very well, but the three towered over the short foreman like lumbering giants. Or football linemen. I pictured the three of them and a fourth, maybe that Jerry Harris Danny mentioned, jumping out of a van and killing Sarah and Richard while "El Gallo" sat at the wheel. It worked for me. Montero had said the van owner's story sounded hinky.

I picked up my stuff and walked over to the table where they had been sitting. There were several different kinds of cigarette butts on the ground. I didn't know if they were the same types I had found before or not, but I thought they might be. I put them in one of the bagel wrappers.

I should have called Montero right then and told him what I suspected. It wasn't proof. The cigarette butts could prove worthless. I could hear a defense lawyer arguing "Just because my client smoked that brand of cigarette and was often in Riverside Park is no reason to assume he committed these tragic crimes." But the information could help Montero go in the right direction. He was already uncomfortable about the van theft. It was his job to check out these guys and arrest them if he could. From a cop's point of view, I had done enough.

Fuck that. Montero would have to wait. I wasn't sharing until I had real proof and found the bastard these creeps worked for and why. I didn't want to scare off my prey. It could be Ambrose. He'd been lying about something. If he was behind it, I wanted to nail his ass. Someone stole a possibility out of my life, and that someone was going to pay for it.

I walked south. My car was still at the condo. I wanted to get back here in time to follow "El Gallo" and his crew when they left work. It was only a sixteen-block walk. Fortunately, it hadn't started to rain. The walk was good for me. It helped burn off frustrations. An hour ago, Cheswick and Thornton were the bastards I wanted. I still wanted them. But you don't always get what you want. I hoped Trujillo finds enough evidence to arrest them for Kayla or something else.

Now the Riverside connection and Lester P. Ambrose were boiling within me. I didn't believe "El Gallo" or his crew were anything more than hired goons. I wanted them sent to prison, but I wanted the guy who hired them to pay the most.

I was moving along at a good pace when my cell phone rang. It was Andy Walther.

"I have the information you wanted. Can we meet somewhere?"

"I'm near the South Ferry Transportation Company. We can talk there, if you're free."

"Great. I need lunch. I'll see you in about thirty minutes."

The South Ferry Transportation Company is an upscale restaurant in a restored ferry docked at the foot of Cutter Avenue. When the railroad came and bridged the river, ferry service dropped off. The North Ferry River Service went out of business a century ago. All that remains is its name on a street. The original South Ferry Transportation Company managed to keep a ferry running until the 1950s. In '84, investors bought all rights to the company from its heirs. They raised the last ferry where it lay sunk in the mud, completely restored it, tied it to its berth, and created a wonderful dining experience.

Once a month, in the summer, they take the ferry out for all-day parties on the river. The parties are pricey but worth it. Karen and I went once and had a great time.

I was remembering that day as I drank a beer and watched the water when Andy Walther came in and sat down.

"Bring me a shot of Wild Turkey, a draft, your biggest T-bone cooked rare with seasoned fries and a side of fresh tomatoes," he told the waitress then asked if I wanted anything.

"Another draft. Thanks."

"No problem—you're paying for it. Don't give me that look. I busted tail for this stuff. Who knows when you'll tell me your story or if I can print it? You owe me and I can't afford this place."

"What makes you think I can? So much for favors. You could have ordered the fish special, you know. Let's see what I'm paying for."

"Patience. Patience. Let me have my drinks first."

Andy held the shot of Wild Turkey to his nose and sniffed it. He drank it down slowly savoring the flavor. His eyes were squeezed shut and he shuddered. Then he took a sip of his beer.

Andy's forty with conservatively cut sandy hair. He used to wear it long. He's medium height and build. He wears the same tweed jacket with leather elbow patches he wore when we first met. It was old then. I think he bought it when he became a reporter thinking that was what reporters wore. At least he has it cleaned once in awhile. He used to smoke a pipe. He's worked for the *Daily Record* since graduating from high school. It's all he's ever done.

He reached into his jacket and brought out his notepad and some folded papers.

"First of all, Tri-X Entertainment. They weren't in the news very often until recently, but you know about that. They're a private corporation and they own X-rated video stores. They started with the Triple-X Video Arcade in '89. There were demonstrations for public decency in front of their shops. They won a couple First Amendment suits against the city and no one's proved they're doing anything illegal. The president, Charles Cheswick, manages to separate his public image from his businesses. His name only came up once in connection with Tri-X when they first incorporated. He uses lawyers as public spokesmen.

"Cheswick is an old and respected area family name. For respected, read wealthy. They were early railroad investors. They didn't 'lay rail,' they owned it. Charles is the last of the line, except for some cousins, and inherited that house on River Drive. He belongs to several civic organizations including the Building a Better City Committee and the Police Benevolent Society. He donates to area charities and supports the Fine Arts Museum and City Symphony."

Andy handed me duplicated pictures and articles on Cheswick that appeared in the newspaper.

"Word is Cheswick was considering a run for city council. Probably won't happen now. He and his home have been connected with Gwen Archer and the furor you stirred up. Care to comment?"

I smiled. "Not at this time."

"That's what I thought. That's why you're buying lunch. Riverside Development Company: created two years ago; subsidiary of WorldWide Builders of Toledo, Ohio; bought properties on River Drive to build luxury townhomes. City council very supportive—especially our deputy mayor—and approvals and permits run through the system in record time. Hailed as 'a wonderful and ambitious project for the city's future,' unquote. Run-down area with a lot of abandoned buildings. This project means a lot of money. You won't be popular if you smear them and quash this deal."

There were pictures of Lester Ambrose with the mayor and the city council shaking hands and breaking ground and of old factories and other buildings being torn down. There were accompanying articles. I hadn't heard anything yet that rated lunch at South Ferry prices.

Andy's steak arrived and he ordered another beer. "You don't seem happy."

"Not really," I said stealing one of his fries. I was paying for them, after all. "I was hoping something would jump out and scream 'Hey! This is it! Problem solved!' It's not your fault if there's nothing there."

Andy attacked his steak and I stole another fry. Things were moving along, but I had hoped Andy would come up with something extra. It wasn't his fault, so I tossed him a few bones—besides the one he was currently cutting around.

I told him about Sam's Deli and their picture wall. With Memorial Day and the anniversary of D-Day were coming up, it could make a nice feature. He agreed. I gave him background about the hunt for Linda Miller and the rape of Kayla Barnes and what I knew about the attacks at the Kathouse. I told him to speak with Frank Taylor, Kerri Trujillo and Ed Montero. When things washed out, they deserved the credit.

I didn't tell him about my budding relationship with Sarah Hastings or about what happened at Calvin's place. It wasn't because of my lawyer's concerns; I had already shared my story with five strangers yesterday. It was still too raw. I wasn't ready to go public. That's what telling Andy would be, even if he never printed it.

Andy needed to get back to work. He gave a quick rundown on the deputy mayor and gave me copies of articles and photos. Barrow and his wife, a former beauty queen, came to the city twelve years ago and he joined a local law practice. He got involved in city issues, joined civic organizations and made a name for himself. He was elected to the city council six years ago and was reelected two years ago. The other council members appointed him deputy mayor.

It was nearly two years before the next election but he was putting himself into a good position to run for mayor. It was only rumor he would run; the current mayor was well-liked, and no one knew her plans. Barrow was playing it safe, gathering support, but not ready to go head-to-head against her. Whenever Mayor Durant was out of town, Barrow made opportunities to show he was in charge.

I thanked Andy and said I'd read everything later. I stuffed the papers in my bag with everything else and paid the bill. There went my budget.

Twenty-Three

THE RAIN CAUGHT me three blocks from home. I left the bag with the stuff Andy gave me on the kitchen counter and changed clothes; then managed to drive back to Riverside Park by 3:30. It was now almost seven. It had rained on and off all afternoon, but the light rain hadn't stopped any work at the Bluffs project. Occasionally, I ran the wipers to see better. There was another hour before sunset, and the sky was picking up some color in the west through breaks in the clouds. I debated about going to Sam's Deli or to the public restroom in the park because I needed to pee. It was a tossup as to which was closer. I shouldn't have had a second beer.

I hate stakeouts. They're boring; I always feel conspicuous; and I never know when I'll need a potty break. I'm also afraid that what I'm watching for will happen while I'm on the toilet. Male cops and PIs I've talked with say they usually keep a jar or bottle in the car for such purposes. That's okay for them, but I don't have their plumbing. What do women fighter pilots and astronauts do?

Just as I decided to find a bathroom, a whistle blew and workers began leaving the construction site. I closed the car door, sat back and waited. A lot of the workers came across the street to get their cars from the Riverside Park parking lot.

Others started walking to the bus stop ignoring the rain. Shortly later a white passenger van with a Riverside Development Company sign on the side pulled out and headed south. "El Gallo" was driving. The van looked full. I followed.

Following someone isn't really hard, but it's not as easy as it looks in the movies. If you stay too far back, you risk a bigger vehicle getting in your way and blocking your view. You might miss who you're following making a turn. If you stay too close, even the most casual driver may notice you after awhile. Law enforcement often has the advantages of manpower and budget. They can use multiple cars: leading, following, running parallel on adjacent streets; keeping the suspect boxed. If available, they can have a helicopter overhead.

When you're alone—like me—you just have to stay on your toes and hope you don't have an accident or get pulled over for running a red light. There are just two factors in your favor: most drivers aren't observant about who's behind them; most drivers don't expect to have someone following them.

Following "El Gallo" was not difficult. The white van stood out and traffic was light; rush hour had come and gone. He went down River Drive and turned west on Cutter Avenue. Heavy clouds kept the evening sun from shining in my eyes. At 32nd Street he pulled into a budget motel parking lot. I pulled over to the side of the road. Six workers got out of the van and headed for the rooms. None of them were the three guys I had seen with him earlier. The van pulled out onto Cutter and continued west.

Four blocks later between 36th and 37th Streets, the van crossed over and pulled into another motel's lot. Five workers got out. The three pals of "El Gallo" and two others. The twosome headed for the stairs. The others stayed at the van talking. I had no idea what they were discussing, but they seemed to be arguing. One of them slammed his hard hat into the side of the van, picked it up, and stormed off. He went into a first floor room facing the street. Shortly, the other two went into a neighboring room and "El Gallo" pulled back onto Cutter. I quickly drove through the parking lot of the Sunrise Motel to get a look at the room numbers. The workers were in rooms 106 and 107. I pulled back onto the street and went after "El Gallo."

He turned left onto 66th Street into a modest residential area. A block south, he turned right and went half a block. He turned right into the driveway of a pink-stuccoed bungalow with a small front lawn. The lawn needed cutting. I drove past and parked two houses down. I watched "El Gallo" go into the house.

I took the chance he wouldn't leave before cleaning up or having his dinner. I drove around the block to the Capri Plaza Shopping Center that backed onto the houses where "El Gallo" lived and faced Cutter Avenue. I rushed into the Piggly Wiggly and used their restroom. On the way out, I bought two bear claws and a yogurt drink. I always feel embarrassed going into a store to use their restroom and not buying anything. I can't do it. Besides, this was dinner for me.

I drove back to "El Gallo's" and parked in front of a pastel blue house where I had a good view. All of the houses were of the same design and were painted in washed-out Mediterranean colors. I made myself comfortable, ate dinner, and waited to see if "El Gallo" was going anywhere else.

As I waited, I thought over everything I had learned and thought it was damned stupid of "El Gallo" to use his own van for the attacks. Montero had said the blue van was reported stolen from the owner's driveway. Sixty-six blocks to the crime scene seemed like a long haul, to me, for just anyone wanting a getaway vehicle. It had to be "El Gallo" and friends.

I waited until 11:45. "El Gallo" never left, no one came to visit, and no one called the cops about a stranger sitting in a strange car parked in front of their house. The lights at "El Gallo's" had gone out at 10:15. This had turned into a wasted night.

I didn't know "El Gallo's" last name or his phone number. There were ways I could get it. The easiest one being to call Detective Montero and ask for it. But I was avoiding Montero. He'd ask questions I didn't want to answer. I had the address, so I could go online and get the number through a reverse look-up — if it wasn't unlisted. But that required going home. I wanted to confront "El Gallo" now. Shake him up and see what happened. I was frustrated and I wanted him to be frustrated too.

I debated about just walking up and ringing his bell and telling him my thoughts just to see what would happen. Instead, I drove to the Sunrise Motel and parked on the other side of Cutter where I could see the rooms in front. I called directory assistance and then the motel. An automated answering system told me to dial the room extension I wanted or zero for the motel manager. I punched in 107. That was the room the upset worker went into. I thought I'd upset him some more.

His voice was groggy when he answered, as if he had been asleep or was drunk.

"'Ello, luv." I said, badly imitating an English accent. "This is Sarah. Why did you guys kill me?"

I hung up. If I were wrong about these guys, nothing would happen. On the other hand —

The door to 107 flew open. The guy came bursting out wearing only a pair of Jockey shorts. He looked like Charles Atlas in one of those ads you used to see on the back of comic books. The after shot, not the 98-pound weakling. This guy was big, at least six-four. He was broad and muscular across the chest and shoulders. He had narrow hips. The muscles in his arms and legs were well defined in the angled light. He banged on the door to room 106. I could hear it from where I was, and lights went on in several rooms. When the door to 106 opened, he rushed in and the door closed behind him. Half an hour later, he came out and went back into 107. He looked unhappy. He slammed the door behind him. I couldn't call and shake up "El Gallo." Maybe they did it for me.

AT 7:00 A.M., I WAS BACK at Riverside Park waiting in my car. I had coffee and bagels from Sam's. The sky was clear. Some workers had already arrived. At 7:45, "El Gallo" arrived with his van full of workers. At 8:00, Shirley arrived in the Ford Taurus and opened the office. Lester Ambrose arrived at 9:30. "El Gallo" went into the office at 9:45. He came out again at 10:00 slamming the door and making a pointed gesture. Five minutes later, Ambrose stormed out, got into his Lexus, and rushed off. My, my. Things were starting to happen.

I followed him north on River Drive. It's four lanes, but the speed limit is only 45 mph. Ambrose was doing over 60. I was afraid one of us, or both, would get ticketed. He didn't slow down until we got onto North River Drive where the wealthier neighborhoods were. He must have realized that area was patrolled more often. Was it possible he was headed for Cheswick's place? As much as I would have liked there to be a connection, it wasn't highly likely. As far as I knew, Cheswick was still out of the country.

A mile south of Cheswick's, Ambrose turned off to the left, away from the river, into a well-to-do but not rich rich neighborhood. The homes here were spacious with manicured one or two acre lots. The streets were wide and meandered in sweeping curves. I felt out of place. I was sure the nannies and gardeners drove newer and better cars than I did. It was the kind of area I might consider if I won the lottery.

Ambrose made a couple of more turns and pulled into a cul-de-sac. I waited at the corner. Ambrose drove into a drive at the end. Tall neatly trimmed hedges and evergreens screened the yard. I could see the top of a two-story Tudor-styled house. I pulled into the street and up to the drive. Even from there I couldn't get a look at the house. The drive was circular and more tall hedges blocked the view. There was no name on the mailbox. I took down the address. I didn't know if it was Ambrose's house or if he was visiting someone. I'd find out later.

I drove back to Riverside Park and walked across to the Bluffs. I signed in with the guard and went to the office. The secretary was alone.

"Hi. You're Shirley, aren't you? I was here the other day speaking with Mr. Ambrose. Is he here?"

"I remember you. No, I'm sorry, Mr. Ambrose left a little while ago."

"Do you expect him back soon?"

"I don't know. He didn't say. He had an argument with his foreman and they both left like the devil was chasing them. Say, can I ask you a personal question?"

"Sure."

"Are those breast implants?"

"No, they're all me I'm afraid."

"Wow. You must get hit on by guys all the time."

"More often than I care to be."

"I was thinking of getting implants. You know, to make the guys notice me a little more. What do you think, is it worth it?"

"No, I don't think so. These are heavy and they put a strain on my back and neck. I have to have clothes specially fitted, especially my bras. As I get older, they'll droop and cause me other problems. I'm saving for breast reduction surgery. Truth to tell, when I came in the other day, I was really envious of your breasts. I still am."

"Really? Wow. I never thought about it like that. Seems all guys want are big tits."

"Yeah, but guys don't have to wear them. We do."

Big breasts are a plague and a curse. I don't understand why any woman would want to be saddled with them. I'm getting rid of mine as soon as I can. There's nothing like a little honest girltalk and an admission of envy to build rapport. Share a secret with someone and they'll tell you their life

---

190

history and just about anything else whether you want to know or not.

"You said Mr. Ambrose was fighting with his foreman. Was that the same one he was arguing with the other day? Nick . . . ah . . . I don't recall his name."

"Nick Guerrero. Yeah, that's him. The past couple of weeks all they do is argue. They were really going at it this morning. The walls were shaking."

"Problems with the project?"

"I don't think so. Everything's on schedule from what I hear. This was something personal. I think it had to do with family."

"What makes you think that?"

"Well, they kept mentioning Mr. Ambrose's brother-in-law. From other things I've heard, I think they all used to be friends back in Ohio. I don't know what the problem is, but it's really got the two of them worked up."

"Who's the brother-in-law?"

"I don't know. I don't think I've ever seen him. If I did, Mr. Ambrose never introduced him. Mr. Ambrose and Nick never use his real name. They always refer to him as 'Shorty.' I think that's funny, don't you? Considering how short Nick is."

The name "Shorty" made me wince. "That does seem funny. Have you worked for Riverside long?"

"About a year. I was a typist at the main office downtown, and when they opened this office, Mr. Ambrose brought me out here."

"You have no idea if Ambrose is coming back today?"

"No I don't. Sorry."

"That's all right. I'll catch him another time. And reconsider about wanting implants. I think your breasts are perfect."

I hoped I left Shirley with a new appreciation for her breasts. If she weren't so hung up about attracting guys, I'd offer to show her just how attractive I found them.

I saw the white van "El Gallo" had used. I knew his name was Nick Guerrero, but I still thought of him as "El Gallo." There was no one around. The guard at the gate was facing the street and busy reading. I walked over to the van. I took a manila envelope from my pocket, wrote "Nick Guerrero" on it, and stuck it under the windshield wiper. The envelope contained the article on Sarah's death and her picture from the newspaper. I had written on it "Why, luv? Sarah." I went back to my car.

At noon, a whistle blew and workers began coming out for lunch. I recognized Juan and Danny as they went toward Sam's Deli. I saw the three guys that worked with "El Gallo" come across the street and buy something from the lunchwagon that was there again. They went to the same picnic table they had used before. "El Gallo" wasn't with them.

Minutes later, the white van came out of the construction site, turned south and pulled away in a hurry. "El Gallo" was driving and he was alone. He must have found my present. His three friends saw him and stood up. Then they started arguing. I went after the van.

"El Gallo" drove straight home and went into the house in a hurry. He had the manila envelope. There were no cars parked along the street, so I went to the end of the block and parked around the corner where I still had a view of his house.

Twenty-Four

IT WAS A LONG afternoon and evening. "El Gallo" came to the door twice but didn't leave. After the mail was delivered, a woman came down to the box to get it. She was probably his wife. She looked around; then hurried back into the house. As people returned from work, someone would pull back the curtain at a window and look out. As it grew dark, all the lights were on in the house.

I made two trips to the Piggly Wiggly to use the restroom. I bought a bag of mints and then some cheese and crackers and a bottle of water. "El Gallo" was still home. The van hadn't moved, and I was pretty sure it was him I saw at the windows.

It was nearly midnight. All of the lights were still on. The front door opened. "El Gallo" came out and went to the van. The woman stood silhouetted in the doorway. "El Gallo" pulled out, went to the other end of the block and turned left toward Cutter Avenue. I went straight to Cutter so I wouldn't pass in front of the house. I saw the van at the other corner across the shopping center parking lot. It turned east.

"El Gallo" was scared, I hoped, or at least worried. He wasn't exactly running around with his head chopped off, but he was running. And I wanted to see where and to whom he ran. I hoped I'd get my answers.

The van went down Cutter all the way to the river. It turned right going south on River Drive. Where was he leading me? I expected him to go north to the Riverside site or possibly to the house I had followed Ambrose to.

We were the only vehicles on the road so I stayed back and didn't crowd him. We passed my condo complex, then Lincoln Heights and then we were beyond the city limits where River Drive becomes County Road 1. We passed the place where "El Gallo's" blue van had been abandoned. A few miles further, he slowed and turned left. The road was still close to the river.

I slowed and turned off my lights. As I neared where he turned, a sign read, "Sidney Porter Park, Public Boat Ramp." I looked down the turnoff as I passed. I could see the white van at the end of the road and the river beyond. I saw the lights go out on the van. I couldn't be sure, but I thought there was another vehicle there also.

I kept going then turned around and parked off the side of the road where my car wouldn't be conspicuous. I walked to the corner and started slowly down the road to the boat ramp. I could see the white van like a ghost ahead of me. There was a dark shadow near it I was sure was a car. A dark car. Maybe Ambrose's black Lexus. I stayed to the edge of the roadway keeping on the pavement. I didn't want to be seen, but I didn't want to make any noise tramping in the weeds.

The sky was heavy with clouds. Ambient light reflected from the city didn't help much. I couldn't see anyone. I heard voices but not what they were saying. Suddenly there were flashes of light and brief images of two people followed instantly by three sharp popping sounds. I stopped and ducked low. There was another flash and another popping. It was the sound of a small caliber gun. I heard a car door close and an engine start. The dark car came toward me with its lights off. I moved into the bushes. I couldn't tell what make it was, but it wasn't Ambrose's Lexus. It was just a blur of a black luxury sedan. I couldn't see the driver or read the license number. When it got to the road, it turned right and disappeared. I ran to the van.

"Shit!"

"El Gallo," Nick Guerrero, lay face down next to the van. I couldn't see the three shots that were probably in his chest, but I saw where he had been shot in the back of the head, saw the blood pumping shiny black around the wound. I knew he was dead and that any attempt at CPR was futile. I should walk away. There was nothing to tie me to this crime scene. An early morning fisherman would find him and report it. This bastard helped kill Sarah. He deserved to die. I'd have killed him myself given the chance.

Walk away. Try to catch that sedan.

"Shit."

I called Nine-One-One, gave my location and told the dispatcher there had been a shooting. Then I turned Guerrero over and tried to save whatever life there was in his worthless body. There was no exit wound from the shot to his head. He was still bleeding. Dead bodies don't bleed, no matter what they show you in the movies. When the heart stops, so does everything else. I worked on him the entire time until the paramedics arrived. Thought I still had a heartbeat. Thought I could hear rattled breathing.

I let the medics take over. I had blood on my hands and clothes. I could even taste it from giving him mouth to mouth. I hoped to God he wasn't HIV positive.

I fucked up. I should have called Montero and told him everything I knew or suspected. He would have listened. He's a good cop. He would have done it right. Guerrero wouldn't be lying here bathed in his own blood. I never seem to learn. I had to be the Lone Ranger again. Had to do it myself. I was literally sitting at a dead end.

The sheriff's department hadn't arrived, but I was sure deputies were rushing from somewhere in the county. I heard the distant call of a siren's scream breaking the night. I called Montero at his home number. Better late than never. I told him everything. He listened without interrupting as I blurted on. He didn't chew me out right then; that came later. Then I called my lawyer. I asked her to pick up some clothes and meet me at the sheriff's station. It was going to be a long night.

IT WAS AFTER SIX BEFORE they let me go. It was getting light and the sun would soon be rising. Carmen Andrews, my lawyer, told me to go home, take a shower and get some sleep. I knew she was right. I felt grody and worn out. I wanted to get away. Get on a jet plane and disappear.

I had washed and was wearing clean clothes—Carmen insisted upon that when she first saw me—but I didn't feel clean. The cops hadn't liked it, but they had little choice.

Carmen was waiting when they brought me in. She told them flat out, "Either she gets cleaned up and changed, or there's no interview. She didn't shoot him. She reported it and tried to save his life. End of discussion."

They tested my hands for gunpowder residue before letting me wash and kept the clothes I had been wearing, even my shoes. "Evidence," they said. They just wanted to get a little bit back for my lawyer being there. It was petty schoolyard stuff, but we all do it.

Montero and his partner, Dean Lockhart, had shown up at the boat ramp at about the same time as the detective from the sheriff's department. They explained their interest and he let them stay as he questioned me at the scene. Neither Montero nor Lockhart asked any questions, then. They just listened. I kept my answers short and to the point. I knew they would take me in for further questioning and I wanted Carmen to be there. I wanted someone on my side. From the looks Montero and Lockhart gave me, I didn't expect it to be either of them. Though Lockhart did volunteer to drive my car back for me. I'm sure he searched it.

The interview went on all night. I told my story sixteen different times, sixteen different ways, but it all said the same thing. Montero and Lockhart sat in and asked questions right along with the sheriff's detective. Their questions got down to the nitty-gritty because I had already told Montero everything on the phone. Now he had it officially, on the record, and he could pursue it as far as he needed.

If the questions went in a direction she didn't like, Carmen saw to it they stayed on subject. Like when they asked, "You're an experienced detective; why weren't you carrying a gun?" Carmen interrupted. "She had no reason to think she needed one last night. Your question isn't pertinent to the situation." They may think I shot Guerrero and stashed the gun, but Carmen didn't want them going into the facts that my gun was being held by another sheriff and the neighboring state wanted to extradite me. I was at the scene of violent death a little too often, lately.

In the end, they wrote it down as one Dominick "Nick" Guerrero being killed by a person or persons unknown that may or may not have a connection with the deaths at the Kathouse. That's when the chewing out started. "Bonehead" was the most polite term used. Montero would have still been at it if Carmen hadn't called a stop to it. We waited for my statement in sullen silence. Carmen read it. I signed it.

When I got home, Rasheena and Shoshana were waiting.

"Are you okay?" asked Shoshana hugging me.

"I'm fine."

"When your lawyer called to say she was picking up clothes, we got really worried," said Rasheena. "We called Grandma."

"You shouldn't have done that. She's probably been up all night too."

"We care about you."

"I know. Thanks, but I'm fine. Really. I wasn't hurt. Call PJs and let her know and then go to bed. Please. That's what I'm going to do."

I went to my room and drank three fingers of Scotch, never tasting it. I wasn't fine. I threw everything I was wearing into the hamper and took a hot shower. I scrubbed myself with a small brush everywhere I could reach and washed my hair three times. I still felt dirty. I couldn't reach inside and clean away the guilt. I buried myself in bed and wished the world to go away.

At eleven o'clock, the world was still there. I was bone tired, but awake. I was restless. There was nothing for me to do. The police knew everything I knew. Let them handle it. I had screwed things up enough. I put on a robe and went to the kitchen. Rasheena and Shoshana were in the living room giggling over an old cartoon on the television about some fat kid running around yelling "Hey! Hey! Hey!"

Must be nice. Nice to be able to laugh. I think I remember laughter. Maybe it'll come back to me in the next life.

I poured a cup of coffee. I'd have to get Rasheena to show me how she makes it. She uses the same coffee and the same water, but hers tastes better. I sat beside them on the couch. They looked at me but didn't say anything. The inane banter on the television swept past me, but they seemed to be getting a kick out of it.

My bag and the papers Andy gave me were on the end table. One of the girls must have moved them there from the kitchen counter. I had forgotten about them. Not that they were that important now. I was through. I'd caused enough trouble for one lifetime.

I didn't find the TV show interesting, so I began thumbing through the papers, anyway. They were all photocopies of articles and photographs that had appeared in the *Daily Record*. Most of the gray tones had dropped out of the photographs, but I could see who was in them pretty well. I had gone over most of it with Andy at lunch.

There was the photo of Lester Ambrose with the mayor and city council with their shovels at the Bluffs at Riverside groundbreaking. Deputy Mayor Barrow was at one end of the group. Everyone wore hard hats. There were articles about the project. Andy highlighted everywhere the names Riverside Development Company, Ambrose and Vincent Barrow appeared.

There were photos and articles involving Carl Cheswick and Tri-X Entertainment, Inc., and again, Andy had highlighted the names. One photo showed Cheswick and Barrow together at a Police Benevolent Society dinner. "City councilman Vincent Barrow thanks local philanthropist Carl Cheswick for his $10,000 donation to the Police Family Fund." Unnamed in the background was Gwen Archer talking with the Police Commissioner. The photograph was three years old.

Articles and photographs of Barrow and his wife, Monica, went back a dozen years. She was a handsome woman much taller than her husband. There was an announcement of his joining the law firm of Harris and Moosbrugger. He specialized in corporate law. There were articles of his becoming involved in local issues and running for city council. More recent articles dealt with his tirade for "law and order" and demand for the closing of "dens of iniquity" and "blights of moral decay."

There was one small article on Mrs. Barrow joining the Women's Club. "Beauty queen joins Women's Club. The Women's Club welcomed a beauty queen into their ranks Friday. Mrs. Monica A. Barrow, wife of newly elected councilman Vincent Barrow, became the newest member of the club at its monthly luncheon. Mrs. Barrow is the former Monica Ambrose who was once Miss Toledo and a runner-up to Miss Ohio in state beauty competitions."

("I don't care what my brother-in-law promised you,")
("They always referred to him as 'Shorty.'")
("Shorty thinks he's a real bull")

I began shaking slightly. I went back through the photos of Barrow. I hadn't paid particular attention to them.

Wherever he was standing with a group, he was always in front or at the side because he was always the shortest person in the photo.

There were three more photos of him and Cheswick schmoozing at various functions. One included Gwen Archer. Another the Police Commissioner.

"You shall be known by the company you keep."

There was one other small item: "B&B Investments, Inc., has been established as an 'S' corporation. B&B Investments is a real estate investment company owned by Monica and Vincent Barrow."

"Rachel? Are you okay?"

"What?"

"I asked if you were okay," Shoshana said. "You were talking to yourself." They both looked at me.

"I'm fine. I am really fine. I need to go out. Don't know when I'll be back so don't wait dinner or anything. If anyone calls, take a message."

Twenty-Five

THE HOUSE WAS the Tudor one I had followed Ambrose to. A big house with formal gardens and circular drive screened from the street. A dozen cars were parked in the drive and in front of a four-car garage. I recognized Ambrose's Lexus. Two other sedans could have been the one I saw when "El Gallo" was killed. I vaguely heard music and voices.

A butler answered the door. "Yes? May I help you?"

"Charlotte Grey to see Deputy Mayor Barrow. Miss Archer made the appointment."

"One moment, please."

I tried to imagine Barrow's expression when the butler gave him my message and described me. I called Barrow's home earlier. A servant said Barrow was occupied with guests and asked if my call was urgent. I said it could wait. Then I dressed in Charlotte's tarty best and stopped by my office before coming here.

The door opened and a red-faced Vincent Barrow stood in front of me. He was barely five-two and must have weighed two hundred pounds. I understood why even Guerrero called him "Shorty." He wore an expensive and well-cut dark tuxedo, but the shirt collar was too tight and a roll of fat bulged over the top.

"Who the hell are you and what do you want?"

"Why, Sugah, be nice. I'm heah for your pleasure."

"Get the hell out of here before I call the police."

I held up a nine-by-twelve manila envelope. "But Shorty, honey, Gwen said you would like what I have to offer."

He paused.

"From what I've *seen*," I waggled the envelope, "I know I'm not as young as you prefer, but I *have* what you desire." I waggled my tits.

He looked quickly behind him, then back at me. If his face had been any redder, he'd have been a boiled lobster. His voice lowered but he still growled.

"We can't talk here or now. I'll meet you somewhere."

"Sugah, it's now or nevah. *Someone's* getting these photos within the hour. You might prefer it be you."

He let me into the house and led me down a carpeted flight of stairs to a basement billiard room. We didn't meet anyone. Everyone was at the back of the house or outside. He unlocked a heavy mahogany door at the end of the room. Beyond was a private study with no windows. Barrow locked the door behind us. The sounds of the party disappeared completely. There was only the quiet shushing of the air system.

He went to the desk and I sat on the arm of an overstuffed leather chair. I laid my shoulder bag beside me and opened it. I kept the envelope in my lap. Barrow picked up a phone receiver and punched a single number.

"Chambers, tell my wife I have business. I'll return to our guests shortly. Don't disturb us."

He pointed to the envelope. "Gwen swore she never took pictures."

I smiled because he just confirmed what I only suspected.

"She lied. Calvin was a clevah boy with cameras. He was particularly good with faces."

Barrow leaned back against the desk, thinking. Would Gwen have lied? Would she have taken pictures? His knuckles whitened where he gripped the edge of the desktop. He looked like a trapped badger.

"What do you want?"

"Why, Sugah, what everyone wants. A better lifestyle, of course." I flashed him a broad smile and winked.

"I can give you ten thousand. I have it here. Do you have the negatives?"

"Yes. But not here. Ten thousand is okay for these. The negatives will cost you a hundred thousand."

"You bitch!"

"Yes, I am, but that's the least of your worries. Do we have a deal?"

He chewed his lower lip. "Let me see the pictures."

"Of course, Sugah. But as they say in the movies, first 'show me the money.'"

He moved around the desk and opened a drawer. I dropped my right hand to my open bag. He took out several stacks of bills and slammed them on the desk. He didn't close the drawer. He leaned forward putting his weight on his hands, the money between them.

"Ten thousand dollars. Now show me the damn pictures."

I didn't move from where I sat but held the envelope out. He came around the desk and crossed the room. He snatched the envelope, opening it as he went back around the desk. He pulled the pictures out and looked surprised. He sorted through them quickly.

"What is this shit?"

The pictures were the portraits Roger Burke had taken. For all I knew, Barrow was right about Gwen not taking pictures. I doubted it. Gwen was the type to keep tight reins on everyone she dealt with. She had to be in complete control, always. And she had filmed what she did to me. I thought photographs existed, tapes too, but I didn't have them.

He reached into the open drawer and pulled out a small semi-automatic pistol, but I beat him to the punch. I had my grandfather's .45 aimed at him, the hammer cocked, a round chambered.

I dropped Charlotte's accent. "Go ahead. Point it at me. Give me *any* excuse to blow you away. Please."

He stared me down for a moment then laid the pistol on the desk and moved away from it.

"You can't get away with this, you know. I'm the deputy mayor. The Police Commissioner and a police captain are upstairs right now. You can't steal from me."

"I'm not here to steal from you, Shorty. I'm here to kill you."

I stood and moved toward him. He backed against a bookcase. He looked for somewhere to run, to hide. But there was no place he could get to before I shot him. He looked at the gun on the desk. Like a trapped animal, he wanted to fight back. He weighed his chances of reaching the gun and he looked at the barrel of my .45 and the deadly intent in my eyes.

"You're a crazy bitch."

"Ain't that the truth."

"They'll hear you. You won't get away with it."

"I don't think they'll hear it. I don't care if they do. Whether I get away with it, or not, doesn't matter. You'll be just as dead."

His expression changed. I think he believed me. I know I did. He had to know how badly I wanted to pull the trigger.

"Take the money. I'll give you whatever you want. Don't kill me."

"Why not? You wanted to rape Linda Miller. You're responsible for Sarah Hastings' death. That's the gun you used to kill Nick Guerrero. It's your time to die."

"I don't know those people!"

I screamed. "Linda's the young COW Gwen was holding for you! Sarah was the woman your goons killed at the Kathouse. Killed with Richard Douglas."

I wanted to shoot him. Wanted it more than shooting Archer and Tierney. I didn't need much excuse. Didn't need any. The gun shook. My finger tightened.

"Oral Roberts, Margo Lane, Gary Houseman, George Dunn are just some of the people hurt so you or Riverside could buy the Kathouse. So you could make a few lousy bucks."

I was shaking. "You killed Guerrero because he was scared or wanted more money. Those people upstairs: the commissioner, the police captain, the others. They're your partners. They and you are why Cheswick wasn't raided. You're his unknown partner."

I had no proof, but I knew it was true. All of it, and he was going to pay. I breathed deeply to calm myself; regain control.

"So ask yourself, Vincent, do you want it nice or do you want it *nasty?*"

"You're crazy."

"Nice is you confess to hiring those attacks. Confess that you're responsible for killing Sarah Hastings and Richard Douglas, that you killed Nick Guerrero. Nice is telling everything you know about Cheswick and Gwen Archer and how you and your buddies protected them. Nice is you get to go to jail for the rest of your fucking life."

"I'm not confessing to anything, bitch."

"Nasty is I shoot you. Nothing vital right away. A hand. A foot. Maybe a chunk of calf or piece of arm. Just a bit at a time so you suffer. But for all of the Lindas in the world, I'm starting with your cock."

He covered himself instinctively as I aimed at his crotch.

"I hope you choose nasty. I really do."

"You wouldn't dare."

I fired. The sound echoed through the room. Cordite filled the air. He folded onto his knees clutching himself; his face drained white. Dark stains appeared. His hands dripping. There was the sharp smell of urine and shit. He began to shake, to sob. A quivering, pudgy blob. The bullet went into the bookcase between his legs; I had dropped my aim. He wasn't hurt.

"Last chance, Shorty. I won't miss again."

I put a small recorder on the floor in front of him and started it. There was a brief flare of defiance and hatred on his tear-streaked face; he reached for the recorder.

Once he started, it flowed out of him, purging him. He confessed to things and implicated people I had no idea of. When he was done, I checked the recording to be sure it was all right. I locked him in a closet. He still thought I was going to kill him—I wanted to—but he did as he was told. So I was nice.

I picked up my empty shell casing and checked the bookcase for my bullet. It was buried in a copy of *American Jurisprudence*. I took the book. I left the money and his gun on the desk. I gathered my pictures and bag and locked the door behind me. I dropped the keys into a pocket of the billiard table. No one saw me leave.

Walking to my car I called Detective Montero. He wasn't pleased to hear from me but let me talk. I told him of Barrow's confession and the recording and where he could find Barrow and the gun used to kill Guerrero.

"You better hurry. They're going to be looking for him pretty soon. If they find him before you get here, the gun will probably disappear. Or he might try suicide. I'll wait for you out on River Drive to give you the recorder. Oh yeah, the Police Commissioner is here. According to Barrow, he's into this up to his tonsils. Bye now."

Epilogue

I WISH THINGS happened differently, but they didn't. There's a saying about wishes: "If wishes were horses, we'd be up to our necks in horseshit." Or something like that.

I made a lot of mistakes. Montero isn't pleased, he won't take my calls, but Frank tells me he loved the recording. Even if Barrow's lawyers get it thrown out. They're trying to suppress the confession and the gun he used to kill Guerrero. My interference could cause problems for the prosecution.

I know Montero would have gotten to Barrow eventually. He's a good cop. He and Lockhart were interrogating the three construction workers when I called from Barrow's house. They already implicated someone they called "Shorty" and they weren't talking about Guerrero. I've heard two of them have made deals. The fourth one, Jerry Harris, is fighting extradition from Ohio. He's the one Sarah clawed. She fell and hit her head when he pushed her away.

Barrow's recording may be a problem for the DA, but Andy Walther loves the one I gave him. I had a second recorder hidden in my . . . well, let's just say hidden. I turned it on before I rang the doorbell at Barrow's house. The sound's muffled but you can hear everything. Andy uses it as source material for stories he's writing.

There's an official police investigation: the commissioner, a captain, and Trujillo's boss have been suspended awaiting the outcome.

Monica Barrow claimed no knowledge of illegal activity and has gone back to Toledo. She's cooperating, say her lawyers, and will return if needed. Lester Ambrose is still in charge at Riverside, and the project is on schedule. Like his sister, Ambrose is very cooperative. He may get charged with something, but it's doubtful.

Cheswick and Thornton have been indicted for child pornography, money laundering and various conspiracies. They're fighting extradition from wherever they are.

Seven bodies have been found so far at Calvin Tierney's place. Not all of them have been identified. None match anyone in my files, thank God. Because of the bodies and the exposure of the child pornography scheme, charges against me were dropped and Rodecker and his detectives received commendations. However, it's been made plain I'm not welcome across the river.

Barrow is out on bail. Apparently he still has influence. His lawyers claim he's being framed by "undesirable elements" in the community. That would be me, specifically, the whole gay community in general.

I hope Barrow goes against his lawyers' advice; I hope he stops fighting the confession and cops a plea. I hope he chooses to be nice and go to jail. I sent him a message, "Dear Shorty, Don't choose Nasty," along with a bullet from my grandfather's gun painted silver. Maybe I am the Lone Ranger.

I still feel guilt over all the deaths—even Gwen's and Calvin's, despite what they did to me. The trauma of my rape is getting less vivid thanks to Dr. Howard and my survivor sisters. Late night calls with Margo help me sleep.

EXCEPT FOR TABLE ONE, the tables in my office are cleared, the files put away, final reports written and sent out.

All that's left is the file on Karen. Everything I've gleaned and found out about where she went and what she did after she left me. I haven't had a new lead in months. It doesn't contain any real answers. Maybe there aren't any. I still don't know why she left. I still love her—I think I always will—but it's time to put her away, too. Stop living in the past and what might have been. Let Karen live whatever life she wants.

I put the file in the closet cabinet and locked the door, picked up the phone and dialed.

"Hey, Frank, you want to go to Charlie's for lunch?"